WILDER BOYS

WILDER BOYS

BRANDON WALLACE

ALADDIN

NEW YORK LONDON TORONTO SYDNEY NEW DELHI

ALADDIN

An imprint of Simon & Schuster Children's Publishing Division
1230 Avenue of the Americas, New York, New York 10020
This Aladdin hardcover edition May 2015
Text copyright © 2015 by Hothouse Fiction
Jacket illustration copyright © 2015 by Thomas Flintham
All rights reserved, including the right of reproduction
in whole or in part in any form.
ALADDIN is a trademark of Simon & Schuster, Inc., and related logo
is a registered trademark of Simon & Schuster, Inc.
For information about special discounts for bulk purchases,
please contact Simon & Schuster Special Sales at 1-866-506-1949
or business@simonandschuster.com.
The Simon & Schuster Speakers Bureau can bring authors to your live event.
For more information or to book an event, contact the Simon & Schuster Speakers Bureau
at 1-866-248-3049 or visit our website at www.simonspeakers.com.
Jacket designed by Karin Paprocki
Interior designed by Mike Rosamilia
Interior illustrations by Jon Howard
The text of this book was set in Alright Sans.
Manufactured in the United States of America 0415 FFG
2 4 6 8 10 9 7 5 3 1
Library of Congress Control Number 2014956672
ISBN 978-1-4814-3264-1 (hc)
ISBN 978-1-4814-3265-8 (eBook)

To Cowboy State readers—
Wyoming's genuine Wilder boys and girls

With special thanks to
Sneed B. Collard III

1

Splashing through murky pools of rainwater by the side of the road, the mud-splattered school bus rumbled to a stop. With an eager leap, Jake and his younger brother, Taylor, rose from their seats.

"Last day of school tomorrow." Taylor grinned at the bus driver as he reached the door. "What are you gonna do without us?"

Mr. Polanachek grunted. "I'm going to get some peace and quiet, that's what!"

"Aw, admit it," Taylor said. "You're gonna miss us, aren't ya?"

"Like I'd miss this ulcer you kids been givin' me."

Jake nudged his brother from behind. "Quit being a pain, Taylor. You're making everyone late."

Taylor laughed and hopped down the bus steps. "See ya tomorrow, Mr. Polanachek! Don't forget to bring your ulcer with you!"

Jake jumped down beside him on the gravel-strewn side of the road. "Do you even know what an ulcer is, Taylor?"

Taylor ran his fingers through his wavy light brown hair and rolled his eyes up at Jake. At thirteen, Jake was only two years older than his brother, but that didn't stop him acting like he was a know-it-all adult sometimes. However, before Taylor could answer, the boys heard a sharp high-pitched bark and saw a brown-and-white flash streaking toward them.

"Cody!" Taylor shouted, and squatted down to let the Jack Russell terrier leap into his arms. "How's our boy?"

The dog squirmed happily in Taylor's grasp and plastered slobber across his cheek.

Jake laughed. "He's right on time!" Cody danced around the boys' feet as if they'd been away for years, rather than a few hours. He always seemed to know the exact time they'd return from school.

As they did every day, the two brothers and Cody turned down a side street into their neighborhood, strolling home to check on their mom. Taylor happily splashed through puddles in the broken sidewalk and kicked a rock toward a peeling yellow fire hydrant that had been almost completely swallowed by weeds.

"I can't *believe* tomorrow is the last day of school!"

Taylor exclaimed. "Man, I can't wait. I'm just gonna sleep in, play baseball, and forget about homework. Hey! Maybe you and me can go fishin'?"

Jake raised an eyebrow at him. *"Fishing?"*

"Why not? Dad taught you, didn't he? I mean, before he left?"

"Well, sort of, but we don't have any gear."

"We can get some."

"How? Do you have money to buy fishing tackle?"

"Maybe Bull will get it for us."

"Taylor, get real." Jake huffed as the blast of a train whistle sounded from the freight yards down by the river. "When's the last time Bull bought us anything?"

Taylor shrugged. "It was just an idea."

Jake kept quiet. The truth was, thinking about summer made his stomach feel like it was filled with gravel. Even though his school wasn't exactly a five-star academy, Jake loved going there every day. He often spent lunch period in the library, devouring books. He hung out mostly in the action-adventure section, but he would read almost anything else in the library too. School was the one place he didn't have to worry about Mom or her psychotic boyfriend, Bull.

"Hey!" Taylor blurted, pulling Jake from his thoughts. "Check it out!"

Jake halted and followed Taylor's pointed finger, sweeping his dark hair away from his eyes. A brilliant yellow-and-black bird perched on a telephone wire less than thirty feet from where they stood.

"Geez, you ever seen one like that?"

"No," Jake admitted. Crows, pigeons, and sparrows ruled the area around their neighborhood. He recognized all of them, but there was normally never anything this flashy. "Maybe we'll find it in the book Mom gave us," he said. "Let's look it up when we get home."

As the boys approached the neighborhood church, they spotted a black-and-white police cruiser parked on the street. Jake recognized the large, familiar shape of Officer Grasso.

"Hey, Officer Grasso!" Taylor shouted. "How many bad guys you catch today?"

The policeman grinned. "Not enough, as usual. How you boys doing? Only one more day of school, huh? You looking forward to summer?"

Taylor gave an exaggerated sigh. "You can say that again."

Jake just nodded. Both he and his brother liked the policeman. Once or twice a week, Officer Grasso would park here, a toothpick in his mouth, to greet the kids coming home from school. The neighborhood had a reputation for petty crime and drug use, and the policeman knew it made people feel safer to see him around.

"What are you going to do with all your free time?" Officer Grasso asked.

"We were just talkin' about that," said Taylor. "I'm gonna play baseball, and me and Jake are goin' fishing."

"Fishing, huh? Good idea. When I was a kid, the rivers around here were so dirty from the factories, we didn't dare go near 'em. Now I hear they hold bass tournaments in them!"

While Taylor tossed a stick for Cody, Officer Grasso lowered his voice and turned to Jake, asking, "Say, you seen Bull lately?"

"Uh, he's been around," Jake answered. "Why?"

The officer had asked the question casually, but Jake picked up an undercurrent beneath his words. Jake had to be careful with these kinds of situations. The fact was, he was afraid of Bull, but he couldn't let anyone know anything was wrong—least of all the cops. Although he would have liked nothing better than to see his mom's boyfriend thrown in jail, Jake knew that if he took a wrong step, Bull would come after him. Even worse, he might go after Taylor or their mom.

The policemen shrugged. "Oh, nothing, really. There was an, uh, *incident* last night not far from here. I thought maybe Bull might know something about it."

Or did it himself, Jake thought.

"Did anyone get hurt?"

The officer lifted his hat, ran his hand over his thick sandy hair, and replaced the hat. "Not this time."

"Well, Bull was home with us last night," Jake lied. "I doubt he'd know anything."

Before the policeman could ask anything else, Jake said, "We'd better go check on our mom."

Officer Grasso seemed unconvinced, but he let the boys go. "Okay. You take care now."

"You too," said Jake, continuing down the street. "C'mon, Taylor. Cody."

Jake felt dread in the pit of his stomach. He hated lying to Officer Grasso, but he couldn't take any chances where Bull was concerned. He had to keep his family safe. Jake and Taylor had lived in this neighborhood for the last seven years, ever since their father left. It wasn't exactly mansion heights, but it was still a tight community. Gossip spread quickly. About four blocks deep by ten blocks long, the neighborhood was lined by simple clapboard houses that had seen better days. For Jake and Taylor, it wasn't much, but it was home.

A couple of houses down the boys passed the peach-colored house belonging to Mrs. Sanchez. As usual at this time of year, Mrs. Sanchez busied herself in the front yard, tending her small vegetable garden.

"Hi, Mrs. Sanchez," Jake greeted her.

She straightened her back, wincing slightly from arthritis. "Oh, hi, boys. How are you?"

Taylor and Cody hurried over to her. "Anything comin' up yet?"

"You mean apart from your bean pole of a brother?" Mrs. Sanchez flashed a wry smile at Jake, who was starting to look a lot older than his thirteen years. "Well, yes, as a matter of fact."

Mrs. Sanchez pointed to a half dozen fat twin leaves that had just poked up out of the ground.

"Cool! What are they?" Taylor asked.

"Don't you remember? I showed them to you last year," said Mrs. Sanchez. "Take a guess."

"Uh, carrots?"

"Nope. Jake?"

"Hmm . . ." Jake had seen the plants before, and he knew the answer was lodged somewhere in his brain. Finally he said, "Squash?"

Mrs. Sanchez beamed. "Very good. Just for that, I'll let you have the first one that gets ripe!"

"Aw," Taylor said, disappointed.

Jake punched him in the shoulder. "If you quit being such a pain, I might even share."

Mrs. Sanchez laughed, then said, "Jake, how is your mom doing?"

"Good," Taylor answered for him. "The nice weather's making her feel like her old self."

Jake knew that wasn't exactly the truth, but he didn't see any point in contradicting his younger brother.

Mrs. Sanchez nodded. "Well, you let me know if there's anything I can do."

"Thanks!"

At the end of the block, the boys approached their own

place—a small house about twice as big as Mrs. Sanchez's. Unfortunately, it was twice as shabby, too—at least since their mom had gotten sick. White paint peeled like dead skin from the wooden siding, while the wooden slats of the fence had begun to fall off one by one. Every year, Bull promised to get the place fixed up and painted, but like most of Bull's promises, this one never amounted to anything.

Maybe I'll just do it myself this summer, Jake thought as he pulled open the screen door and entered the house.

The boys let their book-filled packs plunk to the floor, and then they tiptoed back to check on their mom. The dusty, yellowed blinds were drawn in her room, but even in the dim light, Jake could make out his mother's sleeping form and hear her ragged breath. A dozen orange vials of pills, half of them with their caps off, sat on the small table next to her bed.

Their mom, Jennifer, had never told the boys exactly what was wrong with her, but Jake had overheard the words *depression* and *anxiety*. It had started four years earlier, about the time Bull had shown up. Since then she'd grown steadily worse. First she'd had to quit her job at the bank. Then she stopped being able to go out. For the last year she'd spent most of her time in bed.

For the millionth time, Jake wondered how different it might have been if their father, Abe Wilder, had stuck around. And for the millionth time, anger boiled up inside him. If their father hadn't been so selfish, Bull wouldn't be in their lives. Most of all, their mother might not be sick.

"C'mon," Taylor said. "Let's see if there's anything to eat."

Shaking off his anger, Jake followed his younger brother into the kitchen. Taylor yanked open the refrigerator. "Whoa! Look here!"

Usually, the fridge held nothing but Bull's beer and maybe a half-empty ketchup bottle. Today a fresh pack of hot dogs sat on the middle shelf.

"Looks like Bull used mom's food stamps to buy some real food for once," Jake said.

"I saw 'em first!"

Taylor grabbed the package and tore it open. He shoved one of the cold hot dogs into his mouth and gave another one to Cody.

Just then the boys heard the front screen door open, followed by heavy footsteps. A moment later the scraggly, unshaved face of their mother's boyfriend appeared in the kitchen door. Jake's stomach dropped as Bull's gray eyes flashed toward him.

"Hey, Bull," Taylor said. "Thanks for getting us the—"

Bull's face contorted with rage. "What do ya think you're doin'? Those franks aren't for you punks. And they're especially not for your mangy mutt!"

Bull kicked at Cody, but the dog deftly leaped to the side, cowering from the stocky, barrel-chested brute standing over him.

"Leave him alone!" Taylor hollered. "He didn't do anything to you!"

"He's eating my food!"

"Taylor . . . ," Jake began, trying to calm his brother. Jake knew that once Taylor got going, there wasn't much that could stop him. Even though fights with Bull only ever ended one way.

"It's our mom's money that bought this food!" Taylor shouted at Bull. "Cody can have as much as he wants!"

"You'd better watch your mouth," Bull snarled, stepping forward.

Taylor didn't back down; instead he puffed his chest out and glared up at Bull, his green eyes flashing. "Why? You're not even part of this family! If our dad were here, he'd kick you out on your butt!"

Bull's face grew even redder, all the way up his veiny forehead to the roots of his slicked-back hair. "Thank God, I ain't your dad. Your dad was a worthless loser, and crazy, too! What kind of man would leave his kids and his sick wife to go chase some crazy daydream?"

"She wasn't sick before you came along!" Taylor shouted back. "*You* made her sick. You make *me* sick. You steal and cheat and . . ."

Bull took another step forward. "Why, you lyin' little—"

Bull raised his hand to strike Taylor, his sinewy forearm slick with sweat.

"No!" Jake shouted, leaping in front of Bull's arm as it

began to swing. The blow caught Jake flush on the cheek, knocking him to the floor. Cody began barking furiously. Jake saw purple spots but struggled to get back up, afraid Bull would strike Taylor next. However, instead of continuing the attack, Bull just glared at the two boys.

"You thieving little punks. If it wasn't for your . . ."

Bull didn't finish the sentence. Instead he spun around and stormed out of the house, tearing off the screen door as he left.

2

Cody whined and rushed over to lick Jake's cheek. A pinkish blotch was already forming, clashing with his deep blue eyes; his dark hair was plastered across his face.

"Are you okay?" Taylor asked, helping his brother to his feet. "You didn't need to do that. Cody and me could've taken him."

Jake didn't bother responding to that; he just pushed back his hair and stared at Taylor. Despite Taylor's enthusiasm, neither of the brothers was a match for their mother's boyfriend. And Jake might look older, but he was still only thirteen.

"I'm okay," Jake muttered, but inside he felt an all-too-familiar mix of anger and helplessness at having to put up with a thug like Bull. "C'mon," he said, trying to change the subject. "Let's look up that bird we saw earlier."

Taylor picked up the hot dog package and shoved another one into his mouth. He held the package out to his brother. "You want one?"

Jake couldn't help cracking a smile. "Might as well. My face already paid for it."

Taylor laughed and handed one of the cold wieners to Jake, and for good measure, fed another to Cody, too.

Back in their room, Jake pulled out their bird book and passed it to his brother. The book had been a gift from their mother the Christmas before, and it was already full of dog-eared pages and highlighted passages.

"What do I look for?" Taylor asked, plopping down on his bed.

Jake thought about it. Even though his mom had some-how managed to send the boys to camp the previous sum-mer, and one of the counselors had taken them birding several times, Jake had always gotten mixed up trying to identify the songbirds. "Not sure," he told Taylor. "Try war-blers or finches."

While Taylor and Cody flipped through the bird book, Jake's eyes landed on his dad's old journal, and he pulled it off the shelf. He sat down on his own bed and began leafing through it.

As angry as he often felt toward his dad, Jake prized this journal more than anything else he and Taylor pos-sessed. Their hands had worn the leather cover smooth, but the precious contents remained protected. The journal contained a strange hodgepodge of entries: notes from his father's travels through Wyoming as a young man; sketches of birds, reptiles, and mammals from right here in Pennsylvania; hunting and fishing tips; a section on medicinal and useful plants in the West. More than anything, the journal contained their father's dreams of finding his own kind of utopia, a place where he and his family could live off the land. Clearly, Abe had been obsessed with finding the perfect place.

"I think I found it!" Taylor said.

"What?"

Jake crossed over to his brother's bed. Setting down their dad's journal, he looked at the page Taylor pointed to in the bird book. "American goldfinch, huh?"

"Yeah, I think we saw the male," said Taylor.

Jake took the book and quickly flipped through the warbler section. Then he flipped back to the goldfinch. The picture on the page definitely had the same gold-and-black colors they'd seen on the bird earlier. He smiled. "I think you're right. And I thought I knew them all around here!"

Taylor grinned, but the smile faded when he saw their dad's journal.

"Jake?"

"What?"

"Do you think Dad really *was* crazy? Like Bull said?"

Jake lowered the bird book and paused. Part of him *did*

wonder if his father had gone nuts. Mostly, though, he just thought his dad was selfish.

What else would make him leave his family like that?

"No," he told Taylor. "I don't think Dad was crazy. I think he . . . he just had an idea he couldn't let go of."

"You mean going out West to 'live off the land'?"

Jake nodded.

"But why wouldn't he take us, Jake? Why did he have to leave?"

Jake sat down next to him and shrugged. "I don't know, Taylor."

Just then they heard a tap on the door.

Taylor got up to open it. Their mother stood there, leaning against the doorframe for support.

"There are my boys," she said, her mouth spreading into a weak smile.

"Mom!" Taylor gave his mother a hug.

"Mind if I sit?" she asked.

Jake quickly slid their father's journal under Taylor's pillow and got up to help their mother over to his brother's bed. The boys perched on either side of her, while Cody leaped up and circled twice before resting his chin in Jennifer's lap.

"So," she asked, stroking the dog's head. "How was the second-to-last day of school?"

"Good," Taylor said. "No homework!"

Both Jake and his mom laughed.

"I checked out some extra books from the library," Jake told her.

"It's too bad they can't keep it open for you—" Jennifer stopped midsentence and reached up to touch the red mark on Jake's cheek. Even as sick as she was, concern etched her face. "What happened to you?"

"He—" Taylor began, but Jake cut him off.

"I ran into a metal post at school."

Jennifer might be depressed, but she wasn't stupid. "Who did this, Jake?"

"Uh, I had a little disagreement with someone. My face got in the way of his hand."

Jennifer lowered her own hand, and her body seemed to slump.

"It was nothing," Jake quickly assured her, putting his arm around her back for support.

Jennifer didn't respond, just breathed wheezily in and out. Finally she said, "Promise me, boys . . . that you will try to be good. And promise me you'll try to get along with Bull."

"Why? We all know he's no good!" Jake hissed.

Jennifer's eyes met Jake's. "He's the only thing we've got right now," she said softly. "We're lucky to have a man around here at all."

"Why? So he can spend your disability checks and use your food stamps to buy pizza for his friends?"

Jennifer dropped her eyes. "No, not for that."

"Then what?" Taylor asked.

"Because," their mother said, "we don't have anyone else."

"But we don't *need* anyone else," Taylor insisted. "You, me, and Jake would do fine by ourselves. Jake and I could take care of you until you get better."

Jennifer managed a smile and kissed her younger son on the top of his head, ruffling his wavy hair. "I know you could, but . . ."

"But what?"

Jake guessed what his mother was thinking—that she might get even sicker—but he didn't dare say it. Instead he said, "You should get back to bed, Mom. Come on, Taylor. Gimme a hand."

The short conversation had clearly exhausted their mother. Once they got her back to her room and settled into her own bed, she asked the boys to snuggle up for a while.

"Okay!" Taylor eagerly responded. He climbed in on the far side while Jake sat next to his mom's pillow. Looking down at her, Jake couldn't believe how thin and pale she'd grown in the past year. He swallowed, but it didn't get rid of the sadness he felt—or his worry that she might be getting even worse.

"Tell us about Dad again," Taylor asked.

Jake saw his mother bite her lip, but then she began. "Your father loved you very much."

"I wish I could remember him."

"Your dad was a good man . . . mostly," Jennifer said.

"He knew everything about animals and nature. He could do anything he set his mind to."

"Then why did he leave?"

Jennifer took a deep breath. "He was a dreamer. It wasn't enough for him to make a living. He always had bigger ideas, and when his company let him go . . ."

"That was his chance to go live in the wilderness," Jake offered.

"Yes."

"Is that why he left?" Taylor pressed.

Their mom nodded.

"Didn't he want us to go with him?"

Jake saw his mother again bite her lip. "He . . ."

"He what?" Taylor asked.

Jennifer paused, the conversation clearly taking a toll on her. Then she said, "Boys . . . I need to show you something."

Jake and Taylor glanced at each other, confused.

"Jake, go into my closet and look behind my coat."

Jake got up and stepped over to the closet.

"Under the sweaters, you'll see a box. Bring it to me."

Jake lifted up some old sweaters and was surprised to find a faded orange shoe box. He slid it out from under the sweaters and carried it to his mom.

"What's that?" Taylor asked.

His mom slowly raised herself up. Jake quickly piled pillows behind her for her to lean against.

"When Abe—your father—went out West, he . . . wanted us to go with him."

Jake's and Taylor's eyes met, wide with surprise.

"He wrote to me a lot," Jennifer continued, "pleading with me to take you both out to Wyoming."

"Why didn't we go?" Jake asked.

His mom's jaw clenched. "Maybe I should have," she said. "But I just didn't know if it was right for you boys."

"But why not?" Taylor pressed, growing more agitated. "Wyoming would have been great!"

"Shush, Taylor," Jake said.

Jennifer continued. "Your father, he didn't have a job out there. He constantly moved around. I didn't see how you could go to school, or even how we could survive. I almost got us bus tickets a couple of times, but then I got sick. That made the decision once and for all."

No one said anything for a few moments. Taylor slowly shook his head. Jake was stunned. Finally he said, "What's in the box?"

Jennifer patted the orange shoe box. "These are the letters he wrote to me. You should have them. Maybe they'll answer some of the questions I know you have."

"But why are you telling us now?" Taylor asked.

Jennifer's body seemed to slump again. "I thought it was time. . . . Boys, I'm tired. I need to sleep for a while."

Jake helped his mother get comfortable again while Taylor pulled the blankets up snugly around her neck.

"Thanks," Jennifer said weakly. "I love you, boys."

"We love you, Mom," said Taylor.

Jake opened his mouth to say something, but his mother's eyes were already closing.

"C'mon, Taylor. Let's let Mom rest," Jake whispered.

As he slid off the bed and placed his foot on the floor, Jake felt something slip beneath it. He looked down to see one of the floor tiles had moved.

Great, he thought. *One more thing that needs to be fixed.*

As he bent down to replace the tile, however, he noticed a hole underneath it.

"What are you doing?" Taylor asked, placing the orange shoe box on the floor.

"There's a space here under this tile," Jake whispered.

"Really? Is anything in there?"

"I don't know."

Jake got down on his knees and reached into the shallow hole. He pulled out something heavy wrapped in an old shirt. Feeling the shape of the object under the thin material, he hoped it wasn't what he thought it was as he carefully pulled back the cloth.

"A gun!" Taylor cried, reaching out for it.

"Get off, Taylor," Jake said, pulling the weapon away from him.

"Let me see it!"

"No!" Jake didn't know much about guns, but he did know that they spelled trouble.

"Is that a six-shooter?" Taylor asked.

Jake studied the weapon. It was definitely a revolver of some kind, with a brown plastic grip. Jake saw the words .38 SPECIAL engraved into the short chrome barrel, and remembered reading about those guns in detective novels. He was just as curious as Taylor, but he knew that they'd stumbled across something they shouldn't have, and he tried to make out like it was no big deal.

"Yeah. I think it's a six-shooter," Jake said, wrapping the weapon back up.

"Why can't I see it?"

"Because you just can't, so don't ask again."

Taylor sulked while Jake set the gun aside, and he peered down into the hole. This time he pulled out a large Ziploc plastic bag.

"Money!" Taylor gasped.

Even through the plastic, Jake could see the blurred portraits of Benjamin Franklin and Ulysses S. Grant on bundles of fifty- and one-hundred-dollar bills. First a gun and now cash—it didn't take a detective to figure out what was going on.

"How much is in there?" Taylor asked.

Jake opened the bag and quickly flicked through the bundles of bills.

"Looks like thousands," he told his brother.

"*Wow!* Where'd it come from?"

"Take a wild guess."

"Bull? You mean he's had money all along?"

"Looks like."

"Well, let's take some of it."

Again, Jake's voice grew harsh. "No! And forget you saw it. The gun and this money could get us both killed."

"But, Jake . . ."

"I mean it, Taylor. Just forget you ever saw them." Jake sealed the bag of cash back up and placed it and the gun carefully back into the hole. "If Bull knew we'd found this, he'd . . ."

But Jake didn't have to finish the sentence. Both Taylor and Jake had seen Bull's violent streak more than enough times to imagine the possibilities—and none of them were good.

3

Jake glanced at his mother and then outside, where the afternoon sky had begun to dissolve into dusk.

"Quick," he whispered to his brother. "Put the tile back and follow me."

"Why?"

Jake didn't answer, just picked up the orange shoe box and hurried back to their room, Cody and Taylor on his heels. Taylor closed the door behind them, and they sat down on Jake's bed with the box between them. Cody hopped up and sniffed the box before curling up on Jake's pillow.

Carefully, Jake leaned forward and lifted the battered lid. Taylor gasped. The box was packed with letters and cards with ragged and torn edges, some unopened but faded with age.

"I can't believe Mom was getting letters from Dad for so long," Taylor said, thrusting his hand into the box and pulling out a handful of envelopes. As he did so, half a dozen photographs spilled out onto the bed. Jake picked one up. He recognized younger versions of his mom and dad; they were sitting on a park bench somewhere. Both of them were smiling, and a baby boy bounced on his dad's lap.

Me! Jake realized with a shock.

"And this?" Taylor asked, and handed Jake another photo of a baby, this one dressed up in embarrassing infant overalls.

"That's you."

Taylor's mouth dropped open. "Huh?"

Jake smiled. "Yep. Look how fat you were."

Taylor socked his brother in the shoulder. "Not as fat as you were," he said, peering at the photo in Jake's hand.

But the photos didn't interest Jake half as much as the letters. He picked out one addressed to the boys. It was dated almost seven years ago and, like all the letters, had been postmarked from Wyoming. He removed the single sheet of paper from the envelope and began reading.

"What's it say?" asked Taylor

At first Jake was too engrossed in the letter to respond. Taylor nudged him. "Tell me."

"It . . ."

"It what?"

Jake glanced over at Taylor. "Dad says here that he loves the wilderness and thinks he's heard about some sort of hidden valley."

"You're kidding! What else?"

"He's telling us and Mom that life on the East Coast was killing him—and ruining all of our lives. He says he misses us and wants Mom to bring us out to Wyoming. . . . He even says he's enclosing money for bus tickets."

Jake lowered the letter, and he and Taylor stared at each other.

Finally Taylor whispered, "Jake, Dad really *wanted* us to be with him."

The thought hung like silent fog between them. Jake reached back into the box. "Let's see what the rest of them say."

The boys scoured their newfound treasure. Each letter overflowed with descriptions of Wyoming, and stories of the people there. Much like their father's journal, some letters had practical tips for living off the land, while others shared stories of encounters with wildlife and their dad's own struggles to learn how to survive. However, two themes ran through all the letters: a suspicion about the modern world, and a desperate desire to have Jennifer, Jake, and Taylor join him.

"Why didn't Mom ever tell us?" Taylor asked when they'd almost reached the bottom of the box. Jake looked up to see his brother's eyes brimming with tears.

Jake shook his head. "Maybe she really thought he was crazy. Maybe she thought she'd be putting us in danger, taking us out there."

"But she loved him, didn't she? I mean, why didn't she believe in him? Give him a chance, at least?"

"Maybe she wanted to. But she got sick, Taylor. Remember, she had to go into the hospital?"

"Right after she met Bull?"

"Yeah."

The boys sat there, trying to make sense of it all. Then Jake spotted one more letter in the bottom of the box. He picked it up and saw that it was addressed to their mom, but this one wasn't tattered or faded—this one was clean and recent.

Jake tore open the letter and read it aloud:

DEAR JENNIFER,

I'VE FOUND IT—THE PERFECT PLACE
FOR US AND THE BOYS! TUCKED AWAY
IN A VALLEY HIGH IN THE ROCKIES,
AN AREA COMPLETELY UNSPOILED BY
HUMANS. IT'S THE KIND OF PLACE WE
TALKED ABOUT MOVING TO WHEN WE
WERE YOUNGER. IT'S A PLACE WHERE
WE CAN LIVE OFF OF THE LAND AND BE
AWAY FROM THE HASSLE OF CITY LIFE.

I KNOW YOU GOT SICK OF ME TALKING ABOUT IT, BUT I ALWAYS FELT SURE ABOUT THIS, AND NOW I KNOW THAT IT IS REAL! I'M WRITING IN THE HOPES THAT IF YOU EVER NEED ME, YOU'LL KNOW WHERE TO FIND ME.

I'M NOT GOING TO SEND YOU EXACT DIRECTIONS IN CASE THIS FALLS INTO THE WRONG HANDS, BUT I WILL LEAVE YOU POINTERS FOR HOW TO FIND ME AT A SPOT NEARBY—WHERE I ONCE SAW THE AURORA BOREALIS WHEN I WAS YOUNGER. LOOK OUT FOR THE LANDMARKS I HAVE DESCRIBED, AND I'LL BE THERE EVERY SUMMER, WAITING FOR YOU. I KNOW YOU CAN MAKE IT.

I LOVE YOU AND ALWAYS WILL.
ABE

"Is there anything else?" Taylor asked.

Jake removed a second sheet of paper, and the boys studied it. On it their father had hastily sketched a map of a lake with a waterfall coming down into it. Across the bottom were the words *Teton NP*, along with some notes about leaving inspiration behind them and seeing the aurora borealis. At the bottom of the page was one final sentence: Look across the moose's neck to where the wild-flower falls.

"What's 'NP'?" Taylor asked.

"National park, I think."

"Well, what's this about inspiration—and looking across the moose's neck?"

Jake shook his head. "I guess these are all some kind of clues."

"Not very good ones," said Taylor, hopping off the bed. "But that doesn't mean we can't go find him!"

"What?" Jake stared at his brother.

"Don't you see, Jake? This changes everything. Dad wanted us all to go join him! We can get out of here and away from Bull!"

Cody seemed to agree. He stood up on the bed, his tail wagging excitedly.

For Jake, though, the letters had generated a mix of emotions. Anger. Excitement. Worry. Resentment.

Even if he were looking for a lost valley, Jake thought, *what kind of man would leave us here—and not come back to get us himself?*

"So what do you say, Jake? What are we waiting for?"

"Aren't you forgetting something?" Jake said.

"What?"

"Mom."

Taylor's face suddenly sagged. "Oh . . ."

"We can't just leave her here. Not with Bull. She needs us, Taylor."

Taylor sat back on his own bed. "Yeah . . . you're right. I forgot." Then his face brightened again. "What about after she gets better?"

Jake had never shared their mother's true outlook with his brother. But maybe Taylor was old enough to hear the truth.

"Taylor . . ."

His brother stared at him. "What?"

Jake tried to say the words, but he couldn't get them out.

She's probably not going to get better.

"Never mind," Jake said. "Never mind."

4 Bull didn't return that evening. For supper, Jake and Taylor heated up a can of tomato soup for their mother and helped themselves to more of Bull's hot dogs—cooked, this time. Later, after getting their mom settled, the boys climbed into their own beds. Jake propped up his pillows and plunged into an adventure story by one of his favorite authors, Will Hobbs. Cody hopped onto Taylor's bed and curled up next to his head. Soon Jake could hear the steady breathing of both of them from across the room. He couldn't stop thinking about the map his dad had sent. What did it mean? Finally Jake picked up a pad of paper and began doodling a picture of a moose with flowers around its neck. Then he added the word *Teton* in an arch above it. . . . It still didn't mean anything to him. But it must have meant something to his dad.

After a while Jake turned off the light and lay in his bed thinking about the box of letters, the gun, and the big bag of cash—more than enough discoveries for one day. Eventually his eyes grew heavy, and he drifted off to sleep—only to be awoken with a start a couple of hours later.

"Huh?" he grunted, rolling over to look at their clock. At first he thought it might be time to get up, but the red glowing display read only 4:28 a.m.

Then he heard Cody scratching at the front door.

"Co-deee," Jake moaned under his breath. "It's the middle of the night. Can't you hold it till morning?"

Still half asleep, Jack staggered to the front door, where he found the terrier prancing impatiently.

"What? Didn't those hot dogs agree with you?" Jake asked as he opened the door.

Cody leaped to the ground and sprinted away.

Strange, Jake thought to himself as he sat down in the hallway to wait for Cody to finish his business. The minutes passed, and his eyes were beginning to get heavy once again, but the dog still hadn't returned.

"Shoot," he said, getting up. He went back to his bedroom and, still in his pajamas, pulled on his sneakers and started out of the room.

"Where you goin'?"

Jake looked back to see Taylor rubbing his eyes.

"It's nothing," Jake told him. "I gotta go find Cody. Go back to sleep."

Just then they heard a distant yelp.

"That's Cody," Taylor said, bolting up. "I'm comin' with you!"

"Well, hurry."

Taylor hopped out of bed and shoved his feet into his shoes. The brothers crept outside.

"Where'd the sound come from?" Taylor asked.

"I think down by the jungle. C'mon, let's run."

By the light of a waning moon, the two cut to the alley behind their house and followed it to the next cross street. On the other side of the street, the neighborhood ended, but a single-lane dirt path led through some trees to a small clearing where a lot of people dumped their trash. Neighborhood kids called the area "the jungle." Creeping silently along the track, the boys spotted Bull's truck sitting in the clearing, and next to it, a shiny black four-door sedan they didn't recognize. Suddenly they heard Bull's voice up ahead.

Jake held his finger to his lips. "Quiet."

They kept moving forward until they could make out the dim shapes of two men in the predawn light.

Jake and Taylor crouched down behind a bush. "That's Bull," Jake whispered. He didn't recognize the other man.

"Look, there's Cody!" Taylor hissed.

Jake squinted and saw the shape of their terrier a few feet behind Bull, staring up at both men.

From this position, Jake and Taylor could clearly hear their conversation.

"Bottom line, Bull, you messed up," said the stranger.

"I told you. It wasn't my fault," Bull said.

"What is this? Kindergarten?" said the other man. "It don't matter whose fault it is, you moron. We hired you for the job, and you made a mess of it."

"How was I supposed to know the guy had company? What'd you want me to do: whack all five of 'em?"

"Ain't my problem," said the stranger. "We paid you cash up front to do the job, and you didn't do it. Now my boss wants his money back."

"I—I don't have it." For the first time ever, Jake thought he could hear a note of worry in Bull's voice. "I'll do the job!" Bull said. "Tomorrow. I promise."

"You'd better. *Or else.*"

Something in the stranger's tone made Bull's voice switch again, back to the menacing sneer that Jake knew—any trace of worry was gone. He puffed out his chest and drew himself up to his full height. "Is that a threat?" he snarled.

The assailant stuttered, suddenly on the back foot.

Bull looked crazed, like something had snapped inside him. In a single fluid movement, he whipped out a gun and pointed it at the man. Jake was pretty sure it was the gun they'd found just a few hours earlier. The stranger froze. The brothers looked on in fear.

"You should know better than to threaten me," Bull growled menacingly. "I know how to take care of business."

But before Bull could pull the trigger, a brown-and-white

flash darted from the undergrowth, and Cody leaped out between the two men, barking furiously.

"What the—" Bull cried, startled.

He kicked out at the terrier and spun around in confusion. Even though bushes stood between them, Jake could feel Bull's eyes burning into their hiding place.

"Quick, Taylor, get down!" Jake dragged his brother farther behind the bush. "We gotta get out of here. . . ."

"No, wait. Cody's out there!" Taylor said, gasping.

With Bull distracted, the stranger spotted his chance. He leaped at Bull and tried to grab the gun. The two men spun around in a violent dance. The stranger gripped Bull's wrist, trying to twist the weapon out of his hands—but Bull held on firmly. Then he tried to knee Bull in the groin but missed and hit him in the thigh.

Jake gripped Taylor's arm.

Bull grunted but managed to trip the other man so that both of them crashed to the ground. The bushes blocked the boys' view so all they could hear were the heavy thuds of the men wrestling back and forth, and the terrier barking frantically.

Then, with a sound like a firecracker, Jake and Taylor heard a gunshot. They stared at each other, eyes wide. An eerie stillness descended upon the area, and all the boys could hear was the sound of each other's stifled breathing. The air was thick with silence until a scuffling in the undergrowth brought them back to their senses. Taylor almost let out a yelp, but then he saw Cody emerge from the bushes and leap into his arms.

"Quick, Jake." Taylor gasped. "Let's get out of here!"

Back in their room, the boys piled into Jake's bed with Cody in between them.

"Did Bull shoot that man?" Taylor hissed. Jake could feel his brother's body shaking beside him.

"I . . . I don't know."

"Well, what are we going to do? We're *witnesses*, Jake. If Bull is still alive, he's going to come after us."

"We didn't actually *witness* anything, Taylor. Don't say a word about what we just heard. Not to Officer Grasso. Not to Mom. Not to *anyone*. We can't risk it!"

Jake wished he felt as sure as he sounded, but he saw no point in getting Taylor more worried than he already was.

The two boys lay there for a while, listening for the sound of Bull's return, or maybe the police. All they heard was the distant roar of traffic from the highway, as well as the bellows of a train from the rail yards down near the river.

"Jake," Taylor asked after a minute. "What did that guy mean about Bull 'doin' the job'? It was something illegal, wasn't it?"

"I told you, we just have to forget it ever happened."

"I can't. Bull's mixed up in something really bad, isn't he? Shouldn't we tell the police?"

"Look," Jake said, "I don't know exactly who Bull is mixed up with, but I do know that they're people we need to stay away from."

"So why shouldn't we call the police?"

"Because we don't have proof of anything. Even if we told them what we saw tonight, they might not even believe us. And if they did, we might have to testify—then those people would definitely be after us. They could put us in foster care or something and split us up. We just have to keep our heads down and try to protect Mom as best we can."

"But if we don't do anything, doesn't that make us bad too?"

Jake sighed again. "It's not like it is in movies, Taylor. Real life is a lot more complicated. We have to decide what's the most important thing here."

"You mean Mom."

"Yeah, Mom. We can't do anything about Bull and those guys he's mixed up with, but we can try to stay out of their way and protect her. We have to! There's only one thing Bull cares about, and that's Bull. We have to look out for the three of us."

"And Cody."

"Right. And Cody." Jake smiled, but inside, his mind was in turmoil. He knew that protecting them all would be much easier said than done.

5 The boys rode home together after a restless last day of school. As always, they bantered with Mr. Polanachek, the driver, and he wished them a good summer—but the events of the previous night were never far from their minds. Even Cody seemed quieter as he met the boys when they climbed down the school bus steps.

As they started walking toward their house, Taylor couldn't help but mention what had happened. "Jake, I keep thinking about last night."

"Keep your voice down. I told you to forget about last night."

"But Bull . . . ," said Taylor, kicking a rock in front of him. "What's he going to say when he comes back? What if he's waiting for us right now?"

Jake spun toward his brother and grasped him by the shoulders. "Taylor, I mean it. You've got to forget about last night. We're not even sure that other guy is dead. Bull's stupid, but he's not that stupid. If we haven't said anything by now, he knows we're not going to."

Taylor nodded, reassured. "Okay. It's just I'm . . ."

Jake watched his brother's face crumple, and he loosened his grip. "I know. You're scared. I am too, but it's going to be all right." Jake slung his arm affectionately around Taylor's neck as they continued walking. He hoped he looked more confident than he felt.

As the two approached their street, however, they halted. In his usual spot next to the church, Officer Grasso waited, thumbs curled into his weapons belt. Jake's heart thundered in his chest, and he could feel Taylor's body tighten next to him.

"What's he doing here?" Taylor whispered.

"Just act normal," Jake whispered back, but he knew as well as Taylor did that the policeman rarely showed up two days in a row without a reason.

This has something to do with last night! Jake thought to himself as he and Taylor approached the officer.

"Hello, boys," Officer Grasso said, moving toward them. "I was hoping I might catch you on your way home."

The policeman's voice lacked his usual cheeriness, and Jake knew something was up. "What is it? What's wrong?"

Taylor glanced at his brother and then fixed his eyes on Officer Grasso.

The policeman removed the toothpick from his mouth. "Ah, boys," he said, with a sigh. "There's something . . . Something happened."

Jake waited for the officer to bring up Bull, but instead the policeman said, "It's your mother." The world seemed to slow as the policeman's words filtered through Jake's mind.

Without waiting, Taylor shouted "Mom!" and sprinted toward home.

"Taylor, stop!" the policemen yelled after him, but Jake and Cody were already in pursuit.

As he turned onto their block, Jake spotted two police cars and an ambulance parked outside their house, sur-rounded by a crowd of neighbors, policemen, and medical personnel. The red and blue lights of one cruiser circled silently, flashing an eerie strobe across the scene.

Still in the lead, Taylor headed straight for their front door. At the last moment a large woman in maroon slacks intercepted him.

"Let me go!" Taylor cried, struggling frantically to escape.

Panting, Jake and Cody skidded to a halt next to them.

"Tell us what's going on!" Jake demanded, his mind already zeroing in on the thugs Bull was mixed up with.

What if they came here to get back at Bull and hurt Mom instead?

But just then, the house door swung open. Two men

wearing blue EMT uniforms came down the front steps. Between them, they carried a gurney.

Their mother lay on the gurney, her head strapped into a fixed position. Blood-soaked bandages covered her head—so many that Jake could see only one eye and her left cheek. Even those small parts of her face, though, were marbled with ugly purple bruising.

"Mom!" Taylor broke free of the woman who was holding on to him, and he rushed to the gurney, Jake right next to him.

"Mom, are you all right?" Taylor pleaded.

"She can't hear you," one of the medics said.

"What happened?" Jake asked. "Is she going to be okay?"

Just then Bull appeared in the front doorway. "Taylor, Jake, stop it!" he ordered. "Your mom fell down some steps. They're taking her to the hospital."

Jake stepped forward. *So he's back,* he thought.

"Why didn't anyone get us from school?"

"Wasn't time," Bull barked. "I just found her when I got home. These guys will take care of things. Now, get out of the way."

Tears streamed down Taylor's face. He and Jake watched, stunned, as the men loaded their mother into the back of the ambulance. The woman who had intercepted Taylor spoke gently to the boys.

"I am so sorry."

Fighting back his own tears, Jake turned to her. "Who are you?"

"My name is Mrs. Madeleine Jones. I work for Child Protective Services. I'm here to make sure you have everything you need. We've already talked to your stepfather—"

"Our *stepfather*?"

"Yes, Mr. Duvitski. And we have let him know that we'll support him in any way that we can."

"What do you mean support *him*?" Jake asked.

"Well, with your mother's accident, he'll be looking after you. . . ."

"But—"

Before Jake could protest, Bull walked up behind him. He laid his hand on Jake's shoulder and squeezed until Jake winced in pain. "That's right," Bull told Madeleine. "Me and the boys are gonna be just fine, *aren't* we?"

Jake took a deep breath and stared back at him—he felt like his stomach had dropped through the ground. *Surely, we can't be left alone with Bull?*

Before he could say anything, Bull butted in, "I'm going to the hospital with Jennifer, but I need a word with the boys first."

Uncertainty flicked through the social worker's eyes, but then she smiled tightly and stepped away.

Bull leaned over and looked at Jake and then Taylor. "So, boys," he growled, cocking a thumb back toward the ambulance. "Now you know."

"Know what?" Taylor demanded.

"Know what happens to people who cause trouble and don't do what they're told. I know you was there last night, you little punks. You and your worthless mutt. And I know you saw more than you should've."

"We didn't see anything," Jake said.

"Yeah, we don't know what you're talkin' about," Taylor added unconvincingly.

Bull gave them a grim smile. "You say what you want. I'm goin' to the hospital, but I'll be back in a little while, and then we're going to have a talk. . . ."

With that, Bull walked to the ambulance and climbed in, fixing the boys with a cruel stare. Jake and Taylor silently looked on as one of the paramedics closed the rear doors and walked around to the front seat. The engine roared to life, and the vehicle quickly pulled away.

As soon as the ambulance drove out of sight, a small crowd of police and neighbors swirled around Jake and Taylor. Some, like Mrs. Sanchez, offered their condolences. Tears welled in Jake's eyes, and his throat felt like a boa constrictor had wrapped itself around it. He croaked to the crowd, "We need to be alone." Grabbing Taylor by the hand, Jake tugged him into the house, Cody on their heels.

Once inside, Taylor sobbed. "Jake, what's going on? Why is Bull saying he's our stepfather?"

"So they won't take us away. This way he can keep an eye on us."

"Jake, what are we gonna do?"

Taylor's voice bordered on hysterical. Jake wrapped his arms around his brother, but his mind worked furiously. If they stayed with Bull, their lives would be full of misery—and maybe worse. If they told the authorities, they could be split up, they might even have to testify, and that would be the fastest way to get into trouble with Bull and whoever he was working for. Jake couldn't let that happen—he had to think of a way out, and fast.

Suddenly it came to him—the answer was obvious. He gently pried Taylor loose and brushed the hair from his brother's eyes. "I know what we're going to do, but we've got to move fast."

Jake hurried into their bedroom and unslung his backpack. Taylor followed.

"What are you—?"

"Empty your backpack," Jake said, already dumping his school notebooks onto the floor.

"Why?"

"Just do it."

Taylor began unzipping his pack. "What's happening, Jake?"

Jake met his eyes. "We're getting out of here, that's what. We're going to find Dad."

Taylor's mouth hung open for a moment. "You mean in *Wyoming*?"

"That's exactly what I mean."

"But you said we couldn't because of Mom."

Jake hesitated. He'd never seen anyone who'd been beaten before, but his mother had looked bad. Real bad. *I don't know if she'll survive,* he thought with a pang. "There's nothing we can do for her," he said to Taylor. "But one thing I know is she wouldn't want Bull—or social services—to be in charge of us."

Taylor just nodded, too shocked and bewildered to argue.

"If we can get away from Bull, we'll just end up being separated. We have to go *now*," Jake continued.

"What do you want me to do?" Taylor murmured.

In a pile in the corner of their room, the two boys had already collected some of things they would need for this year's summer camp, but Jake quickly made an additional survival list.

"Pack up what we already pulled out for camp—especially the warm clothes and socks."

Taylor did as he was told. "What else?"

"Get the flashlight."

Taylor retrieved the light from the kitchen, and Jake stuffed it into his pack. Just then they heard someone knock on their front door.

"Boys, are you all right?" came the muffled voice of Mrs. Jones, the woman from Child Protective Services.

Jake and Taylor hurried to the closed front door. "We're . . . We're fine," Jake said. "We just need some time alone right now."

"I understand." Her voice welled with sympathy. "I'm

going to wait outside here. Come out when you're ready to talk."

"All right. Thanks," Jake said, fighting panic.

After a pause the brothers heard footsteps clack down the front steps, and then murmuring voices as the social worker began talking with some of the neighbors.

Jake took a deep breath. "That was close."

"What else do we need?" Taylor asked.

They hurried back to their room, and Jake pulled open the top drawer of the desk they shared. It contained some of his most prized possessions. He pulled out his Swiss Army knife and shoved it into his pocket. Next he handed his compass to Taylor. "Here, you keep this. And go get some string from the kitchen drawer."

While Taylor went off to the kitchen, Jake also pulled a cell phone from the desk. The phone was a disposable one with a fixed number of minutes on it. Jake had seen Bull toss it in a drawer a couple of weeks ago, and Jake had retrieved it when he wasn't looking.

Taylor returned with a small spool of string and put it into his own pack. "What else we need? Can I bring Ziggy?"

Taylor held up the little stuffed raccoon their mother had given him a couple of Christmases ago. Seeing it in his brother's hands, Jake felt bad.

"I'm . . . sorry. We don't have room."

To Jake's surprise, Taylor only nodded and gently

placed Ziggy back on his bed. Then Taylor reached into their closet and held up a battered booklet.

"What about this road map?"

Jake nodded. "Definitely. Good."

"Can we also bring some books?"

Jake glanced at their already-bulging school packs and then walked to the bookshelf. "Only one," he said, selecting their father's journal. Both boys stared at it and then at each other. Jake quickly stuffed it into his pack.

After grabbing a few cans of food and a can opener from the kitchen, Jake led Taylor and Cody to the bedroom Bull and his mother shared. He got down on his knees and pulled up the loose tile covering Bull's secret hiding spot. Bull's gun was gone, but the plastic bag full of money lay undisturbed. Jake grasped it.

"Jake, what are you *doing*?"

"We're going to need cash," he said, straightening up. "It doesn't belong to Bull anyway."

"But you said Bull would kill us," Taylor told him, staring at the cash.

Jake felt something harden inside him. "Only if he finds us. And Bull isn't *ever* going to find us."

Back in their room, Jake also pulled the orange box full of letters from where he'd hidden them under his bed. Jake grabbed the most recent ones and slid them into his bag.

Finally the boys zipped up their packs and struggled into them. Jake could feel the straps digging into his shoulders, but he almost welcomed the pain. It was nothing compared to what he'd felt watching their mother get carried away in the ambulance.

Loaded up, Taylor walked to the front door and peeked through the glass.

"The neighbors are still out there," Taylor observed. "And that social worker."

"We'll have to climb out our window."

They hurried back to their bedroom at the back of the house, and made sure the backyard was clear. Jake slid open the windowpane and dropped both of their packs onto the ground below.

"What about Cody?" Taylor asked. "We're takin' him, aren't we?"

Jake stopped. He hadn't thought about their dog. Almost reading his mind, Cody whined and wagged his tail. Jake smiled. "Of course. We can't leave him with Bull."

Taylor climbed out the window first, and Jake lifted the terrier down to him. Jake dropped to the ground after them. *This is it,* he thought. *No going back.* He picked up his backpack once again, then paused.

"You ready, Taylor?" He asked.

"Ready," Taylor replied.

Together the three of them cut through their neighbor's backyard to the next street over. Then they hurried toward the jungle and away from their old lives. They didn't look back.

6

"How are we gonna get to Wyoming?" Taylor asked.

That's the question, Jake thought to himself. With the cash in his backpack, the boys had more money than they could count—easily enough to buy bus or even airplane tickets, but Jake rejected that option. With or without tickets, the people at a bus station or airport weren't just going to let two boys travel by themselves.

Jake considered hitchhiking, but that was too visible. Anyone could spot them out on a road and report them to the police. He'd also heard horror stories of bad people picking up children and kidnapping them—or worse.

Then Jake thought of another option.

"So?" Taylor pressed.

"Let's head to the rail yards."

"We're gonna ride a freight?" Confusion filled Taylor's voice.

"Plenty of other people have done it," Jake said, thinking about all the books he'd read where runaways and outlaws had hopped freight trains.

"I guess so. . . ."

Jake just hoped that he'd given them enough of a head start on the authorities waiting at their front door. The rail yards lay less than half a mile from their house, and the boys and Cody quickly covered the distance. They followed the dirt track through the jungle, on to an exposed clearing, and back into a brushy strip of trees. There they found a trail that led them to a chain-link fence. They halted. On the other side of the fence, a dozen parallel rail sidings filled an area larger than ten football fields. Freight trains were parked on some of the tracks, but on one, a long train loaded with coal slowly rumbled out of the yard.

"Man, there're so many," Taylor said. "Which one are we gonna take?"

"Beats me."

From the books he'd read, Jake knew that some freight cars were more comfortable than others. He spotted some filled with coal that were clearly no good. On several of the other trains, however, he could see regular enclosed freight cars with open doors. They looked empty from where he, Taylor, and Cody squatted.

"How do we know which way they're goin'?" Taylor asked.

"Will you be quiet and let me think?" Jake said, but Taylor's question was a good one.

Wyoming, that's west, Jake reasoned. *It's not going to do us any good to catch a train heading to Maine or Florida—not if we want to find Dad.*

He looked at the afternoon sun and saw that it struggled to shine through the clouds to his left.

That means that the rail yards run north–south.

"C'mon," he told Taylor. "Let's climb the fence."

The two boys tossed their packs over the fence and scrambled after them. As soon as he saw what they were doing, Cody crawled under a shallow depression to join them.

"Hurry," Jake called, and headed off across the sets of tracks.

"So . . . which one?" Taylor asked, trotting after him.

"I'm not sure, but keep an eye out for guards. They don't like people riding the rails."

The trio reached the first train and ran along it. Jake saw that some of the rail cars were filled with grain.

Grain grows out West, he thought. *So that train's probably heading in the opposite direction—not what we want.*

They crossed between two rail cars to the next train.

"There's an open car!" Taylor told him. Jake followed his brother's gesture to see a pale white metal car covered with graffiti, and they began trotting toward it. They stopped in front of the open door. Inside, the car was empty, the floor covered only by dirty plywood.

Jake nodded. "This could work."

However, as he wandered along the track, trying to work out which way the train was headed, he heard a crunching sound on the gravel below. Jake flushed with panic and stopped dead in his tracks. Stepping out from between two giant cars, a surprised-looking guard with an eager Doberman emerged in front of him. Jake doubled back, eyes wide with fear.

"Quick, Taylor, run!" Jake cried.

Too late.

The Doberman barked at the boys, and the guard hollered, "Hey, you two! Stop now!"

"Move!" Jake said, scrambling under the train, Taylor and Cody on his heels.

"After 'em!" he heard the guard yell, releasing the Doberman.

"Don't slow down!" Jake called to Taylor.

The boys sprinted full speed along the length of the next train, but a loud growl made Jake glance back. The Doberman was galloping after them. As the two boys ran for all they were worth, Cody spun around and charged fearlessly toward the bigger dog.

"Cody, no!" Taylor screamed, but the terrier knew what he was doing. He ran at the other dog, barking and growling furiously. The Doberman was so astonished, it skidded to a halt. Then it seemed to remember how big and fierce it was, and lunged at Cody. Quicker than the big dog, Cody dodged to the side, nipped at the Doberman's flank, and ran past him in the opposite direction. Growling, the Doberman followed.

Jake seized Taylor's arm. "C'mon!"

The boys ducked under another train and, on the next track, found a freight just rolling out of the station. Jake hoped it was moving in the right direction, but runaways couldn't be choosers, and his eyes locked on an open car moving toward them.

"Catch this car!" he told Taylor.

"We can't leave Cody!" Taylor shouted back.

The open freight car pulled almost even with the brothers.

"Come on," Jake hollered, hearing the angry shouts of the guard in the distance. "We have to lose them!"

He pulled off his backpack and then ripped Taylor's off his back too. Carrying both packs, he trotted along next to the moving freight car and tossed the packs through the open door. He glanced back to see that Taylor hadn't moved.

"Taylor, *run*!"

Taylor stood, paralyzed.

"Cody can take care of himself!" Jake desperately shouted.

Just then they heard a bark and saw a small brown-and-white figure racing down the track toward them.

"Cody!" Taylor shouted.

Unfortunately, the guard, holding the Doberman by the collar, emerged just beyond the terrier.

"Stop right there! You can't ride that train!"

"Hurry!" Jake yelled to Taylor. "Don't slow down!"

Both Taylor and Cody charged after Jake.

The freight car was picking up speed every second. Their feet pounding the gravel, the two boys had to sprint to catch up. Jake seized Cody and, with the railroad guard still hollering at them, tossed the terrier into the freight car. Then Jake grabbed on to a small metal handle and swung himself inside.

He spun around to see Taylor running all-out next to the train. Jake reached for him.

"Hurry, Taylor! Grab my hand and I'll pull you up!"

But by now, the freight train was accelerating.

"Taylor! Run faster!"

"Jake, I can't do it!"

"You've got to, Taylor! It's our only chance!"

But Jake just watched in horror as his brother fell farther and farther behind.

7

Suddenly Jake was thrown to the floor of the freight car. The entire train seemed to stagger, and loud crashing sounds filled the air as the couplings of the freight cars slammed together. For a moment he didn't know what happened.

"Jake!" Taylor shouted. "Help me!"

Jake scrambled to his feet to see Taylor's hands inside the freight car door as his brother continued running alongside the rumbling train. Cody stood in the open doorway, barking like mad.

Jake hurried over and grabbed Taylor's forearms. "Jump!" he shouted.

With a desperate gasp, Taylor leaped and Jake yanked him up and into the car. Taylor tumbled onto his brother, sending both of them rolling across the metal freight car floor.

Jake felt Cody licking his face. He and Taylor stared at each other wide-eyed. Then they both burst out laughing.

"Man, that was too close," Taylor said as the train began to accelerate again.

"Yeah," said Jake, sitting up. "*Too* close!"

Taylor scrambled to his feet and peered out the door, back in the direction they'd come. The guard and his dog were disappearing into the distance.

"Do you see them?" Jake asked.

"Not anymore!" Taylor grinned. "Do you think he'll come looking for us?"

"I don't know—but I think we're safe for now."

"Good!" Taylor replied. "But do we know which way we are going?"

Jake joined his brother at the open railcar door. The train seemed to be following the river, and pretty soon they could see the tall buildings of downtown Pittsburgh.

"I think we got lucky," Jake said. "Looks like we're going west."

Taylor grinned. "You think we'll be in Wyoming by tomorrow?"

Jake punched him lightly on the shoulder. "Haven't you paid any attention in school at all? It's going to take us at least three or four days—if this train even goes there at all."

Taylor's grin disappeared. "Are you serious?"

Jake nodded.

They both fell silent as the train continued rumbling

past graffiti-covered warehouses and under bridges. Soon they were passing through the last of Pittsburgh's western suburbs, and brush and forest began to line the rails—running away from home was beginning to feel *very* real.

The boys turned away from the door to check out the inside of the freight car. One end of it stood empty, but six large wooden crates filled the other. Each one had the word MECHANICAL stenciled in large red letters on its sides, and Cody was curiously sniffing the base of one of them.

"What do you think's in here?" Taylor asked.

Jake shook his head. "Engines, maybe."

Taylor placed both hands on one and tried to move it. The crate wouldn't budge. "Wow, these are heavy. Let's open one."

"Leave 'em alone," Jake told him. "We've got enough trouble without damaging someone else's property."

Taylor shrugged and the two of them sat down and leaned against one of the crates. Cody squeezed in between them. The weight of what they were doing seemed to press down on them—even on Cody, who rested his chin on Taylor's knee.

"Do you think Mom's going to be all right?" Taylor asked, rubbing the dog's head.

"Yeah, I think she—"

Jake was about to tell his brother that everything would be fine, but then he stopped himself. He'd always looked after his brother and shielded him from the worst of things, but maybe now he needed the truth. They were in this together, after all.

"Taylor . . . ," he began. "She looked pretty bad. She was already weak to begin with. . . ."

Taylor stopped petting Cody and turned his eyes toward Jake. Jake expected to see tears in his brother's eyes, but instead he saw a determination he'd never seen before.

"Mom's stronger than you think, Jake. Only a strong person could have put up with Bull for the last four years."

"Well, yeah, but . . ."

"I think she's going to make it, Jake. We just gotta find Dad and tell him what happened. Then we can come back and get her."

"Taylor, it's more complicated than that."

"What do you mean?"

"Well," Jake said, now petting Cody himself. "First we have to get to Wyoming—which isn't going to be easy. Then we've got to find Dad, and I don't even know if we can do that."

"Get the journal out," Taylor said.

Jake unzipped his backpack and pulled out the frayed book. Taylor took it from him and began flipping through the diagram- and note-filled pages.

"All these notes and drawings are from western Wyoming, right?"

"Yeah," Jake confirmed.

"So that must be where he's waiting for us."

"Sure, but that's a huge territory."

"Whatever. Look, here he makes a note: *Bridger-Teton*. Didn't you say that's a national forest?"

"Yeah, but it's bigger than Rhode Island!"

"Where's that?"

Jake looked at him. "Are you serious? You don't know where Rhode Island is?"

Taylor grinned. "Gotcha."

Jake punched him in the shoulder. "Very funny."

"So anyway, maybe he's in the Bridger-Teton Forest."

"Maybe. But that could take years to explore by itself. Besides, a few pages later, he mentions Caribou-Targhee National Forest, and a few pages after that, Grand Teton National Park. Dad explored thousands of square miles, Taylor. *Thousands*."

"But we don't have to look through all of it. Dad sent Mom that letter, right?"

Jake reached into his pack and pulled out the envelope. Together they read the letter again, and then they looked at the map.

"See, right there," said Taylor, pointing. "He even wrote it down—Teton National Park."

"Look across the moose's neck," Jake murmured, half to himself. "What does that even mean?"

"Well, there's gotta be a ton of moose in the Grand Tetons, right?"

Jake laughed. "Yeah, but there isn't going to be one moose standing in the same place year after year. No, it's gotta be something else."

"We'll ask for help—whatever it takes, we can make it," Taylor said, determination edging his voice.

"Okay," Jake said. He was tired of arguing. In fact, he was just tired, period. Outside, the sun had set, and the sky had grown to be a dirty gray color.

"Let's try to get some sleep," he told Taylor. "Wake me up if you feel the train start to slow down. We don't want more of those railroad police catching us."

"What would they do to us?"

"Probably send us back to Bull."

Taylor got up and spit out the train door. "Jake, I'm never going back to Bull."

Jake saw the same determination in Taylor's eyes as when he was talking about their mom. Now he felt the same way.

The boys tried to get comfortable behind the wooden crates, and they managed to sleep for a while. A couple of hours later, though, they both woke up. It wasn't the thought of their badly beaten mom or psychotic Bull that invaded their sleep; it was the cold of the freight train. Even though it kept them sheltered from the wind, the car's metal floor sucked heat from their bodies like a meat locker. Eventually, as daylight flickered through the doorway, Jake gave up, and stepped toward the opening. A moment later Taylor and Cody joined him.

"You know where we are?"

"No idea. Ohio maybe?"

Even though trees blocked some of their view, the land was flat, and they could see that they were passing through towns.

Suburbs, Jake thought.

Suddenly Taylor pointed. "Jake, look!"

In the distance, the boys spotted tall buildings reaching above the horizon. Jake recognized one of them from TV.

"Where is *that*?" Taylor asked.

"Chicago," Jake answered.

"Chicago! Oh, man! I've always wanted to come here. Wrigley Field's here, Jake. Do you think we can go see a Cubs game?"

"Taylor, we have to stay out of sight."

"Can't we just look around a little bit?" his brother pleaded.

"I don't know. Maybe," Jake said, shaking his head. "But before we do anything, I've got to get some real sleep. I feel like an elephant was kicking me in the butt all night."

As they drew closer to the city, the train slowed, and the air filled with the smells and sounds of the big city— diesel fumes, traffic on nearby roads, jet airplanes flying overhead, and the sour smells of garbage and trash. Finally the train slowed to a crawl, and the boys saw more than a dozen parked trains in the rail yard up ahead.

"C'mon," Jake told Taylor. "We'd better jump off here."

The boys put on their packs, then Jake sat on the edge of the doorframe and let his legs swing down toward the track. He literally hit the ground running, letting his back foot hit the gravel first, and just about managed to stay upright. He kept running alongside the car while Taylor handed Cody down to him. Then Taylor dropped to the ground too, gravel flying up from his sneakers.

The boys hurried away from the rail yards along a canal, where homeless people had set up shacks of cardboard, corrugated iron, plywood, and even canvas. Some of the shacks were occupied, and a few of the grizzled faces nodded at the boys as they passed, but no one bothered them. That didn't stop Taylor from feeling a shiver run up his back.

"I don't like this place, Jake," he said, running a hand nervously through his hair. "We shouldn't stick around here."

"We won't be here for long," Jake replied. "We just need rest. Otherwise, we'll collapse before we even get started."

Down in the gulley between a railway track and the fence, the boys found a shelter that looked like it hadn't been lived in for a while. It looked like it might be a half-decent place to get some sleep.

"C'mon," Jake said. "Let's crash here for a couple of hours. Then we can figure out our next move."

The boys stretched out on the dirt floor, using their

packs as pillows. A slight chill still clung to the air, but the day was warming up fast, and in no time Jake and Taylor drifted into sleep. Jake slept fitfully, at one moment dreaming of his mom, then the dad he barely knew, and then the nightmarish image of Bull floated in front of him, taunting him.

But then, even worse, the nightmare spilled into reality. Sudden sharp pain erupted in Jake's side. His eyes snapped open. A man with a scraggly salt-and-pepper beard and wild red eyes was standing over them. He held a thick branch over his head.

"Get outta my house!" the man cried as he swung the stick at Jake's head.

8

Cody leaped to his feet, barking, but the man just kicked him away. Jake and Taylor scrambled out of the shack.

"No-good trespassers!" the man bellowed.

"Get your pack!" Jake yelled to Taylor as Cody again hurled himself at the man's legs.

Taylor ducked back inside the shack and seized his backpack.

"Let's get outta here!"

The boys and Cody raced back the way they'd come, following the canal. Behind them, the crazy man yelled, "You'd better run! You come back, and I'll kill you kids—and your ugly mutt, too!"

As they approached the rail yards, the boys finally slowed down.

Taylor looked up at Jake, terror still etched on his face. "Whew, was that guy insane?"

"I don't know. Maybe," said Jake, panic making his voice waver. "We've got to be more careful from now on." Jake couldn't help but think that the encounter might have been much worse. They had barely started on their journey, and they'd already been chased and threatened twice.

"Okay," Taylor agreed, "but right now, I could really use a restroom. . . ."

Jake glanced at Taylor and then at himself. Whatever Taylor's bathroom needs, they both needed to wash up. Their clothes were already filthy from the train ride and from sleeping in the crazy man's shack. Toward the rail yards, Jake and Taylor spotted a large building that looked like it belonged to a railroad company. The boys and Cody hid behind a large Dumpster and checked it out long enough to see three or four company employees in blue uniforms exit the building.

"C'mon," Jake whispered. "Now's our chance."

Taylor picked up Cody, and the three of them rushed to the side door of the building. Inside, they found a long corridor, and from the far end they could hear the hum and shuffle of a copy machine, and the squawk of a radio.

"In here," Taylor said, pushing open a door with a sign that said EMPLOYEES ONLY.

Inside the room, they found several little cul-de-sacs of lockers with benches next to them. Beyond that, they saw four shower stalls, toilet cubicles, and sinks.

"This is what I'm talking about!" Taylor exclaimed, setting down Cody and his backpack and dashing into a toilet cubicle.

While Taylor took care of business, Jake opened their packs and did a quick inventory of their belongings.

"What are you doing?" Taylor asked from inside the toilet stall.

"Just checking what we've got with us so we can decide what to do next."

"So what do we got?"

"Let's see . . . Some cans of beans, Swiss Army knife, extra socks, flashlight, Dad's journal, the letters . . ."

Jake heard the toilet flush, and a moment later the door opened.

Taylor said, "Now we also have one more very important thing."

Jake looked up at him. "Yeah? What's that?"

Taylor grinned and held up a white roll. "Toilet paper!"

Jake laughed and stuffed the toilet paper into Taylor's pack. "Good thinking. C'mon, let's get washed up."

"Let's take showers," said Taylor. "You stink, brother."

Jake gave him a sour expression. "Oh, look who's talking, sewer breath."

"So c'mon," Taylor said, starting toward one of the shower stalls.

Jake reached out to stop him. "No, Taylor. It's too risky. Let's just wash up in the sinks and get out of here."

Taylor sighed. "Okay."

They went to the row of sinks and began washing. Jake pulled off his shirt and scrubbed under his armpits, and Taylor did the same. As they dried off with some paper towels, an overhead speaker suddenly burst to life. The boys stopped to listen.

This is dispatch. Train 661 from Omaha now arriving on track fourteen. Would the replacement engineer please report to the main office? Also, all railroad employees, be on the lookout for two male runaways, early teens, traveling with a small brown-and-white dog. Boys are thought to have boarded at our Duquesne yard near Pittsburgh with unknown destination. They are not thought to be dangerous, but if you see them, report in immediately. Out.

"They're talking about *us*!" Taylor exclaimed.

Jake yanked his shirt back over his head. "Man, that was fast. We need to get out of here—"

Suddenly the boys heard the door open at the far end of the locker room.

"Quick!" Jake cried. "Taylor! Cody! In here!"

Jake and Taylor ducked into one of the shower stalls, and Cody scurried in after them. Jake pulled the curtain closed just as they heard footsteps approaching.

Taylor looked at Jake in alarm and curled his hand around Cody's muzzle.

"Man, glad this shift's over," they heard a deep male voice mutter.

"You got that right. I swear, some of these older freight cars are falling apart."

The footsteps stopped about ten feet away from the shower stalls, and Jake heard what sounded like the spinning dials of combination locks, followed by the sounds of lockers opening. He looked at Taylor and put his finger to his lips, scared to make a sound.

"Hey," said the first voice. "What do ya think about those two runaways?"

"Man," said the second voice. "I'm glad they ain't my kids. If they don't get their legs sliced off by the wheels of a freight car, they'll be lucky not to get beaten up and robbed by some drifter."

"Yeah," the first man agreed. "Hope the railroad police catch 'em before they get in over their heads."

Two metal doors slammed shut, and then the boys heard the men leave the locker room. Jake let out his breath and closed his eyes, relief flooding over him.

"Jake!" Taylor said. "Did you hear what they said? We can't hop another freight now, can we?"

Jake shook his head. "No. And we can't hang around here. Come on."

The boys sneaked out of the building and hurried

toward a busy four-lane road that ran past the rail yard.

"This way," Jake said, crossing the road and heading west.

"Where are we going?" Taylor asked.

"I don't know," Jake said. "I was thinking maybe we could find a Greyhound bus station and buy tickets to Wyoming."

"But, Jake," Taylor said. "If the train people know about us, don't you think the Greyhound people would too?"

Jake's eyes darted nervously around him. "Maybe . . . But I don't see what other choice we've got. We can't *walk* the whole way there!"

The boys continued walking as fast as they could, with Cody trotting swiftly behind them. Jake knew they couldn't wander along the side of the road forever, and was glad when, about half a mile from the rail yards, he heard the deep rumble of an engine behind them. He spun around to see a city bus heading in their direction.

"Quick! Run to that bus stop," Jake said, and the three of them sprinted to a pole with a purple-and-red route marker on it. He checked the map and saw that the route would take them closer to a main station, where they could hopefully get a long-distance bus.

Jake waved at the bus, and it pulled to a stop with a loud hiss. The door opened. The boys paid the fare with loose change and plunked down into some seats halfway through the bus.

"Where are we going?" Taylor whispered.

"Away from the rail yards—that's all I know," said Jake, still holding Cody.

"But what are we going to do?"

"I don't know. Let me think."

However, as the bus rumbled through suburban Chicago, Jake was out of good ideas. *We've got plenty of cash,* he thought, *but if the police are looking for us, our money might as well be more toilet paper.* Jake carefully studied the blocks of warehouses, strip malls, and neighborhoods as they passed through various towns, hoping something would come to him. He felt very far from home, and even farther away from their dad—wherever *he* was.

He sighed. *Nothing.*

After a few miles, the bus crossed over a busy interstate highway with four lanes of traffic roaring in each direction. On the other side of the overpass, Jake spotted a truck stop. He reached over and yanked hard on the cord next to the seat. The rumble in his stomach had made the decision for him.

Ping. The bell rang, and the driver downshifted, the bus lurching to a halt.

"What are we doing?" Taylor asked.

"C'mon," Jake said, standing up, still holding Cody.

He and Taylor hurried to the front of the bus. The driver said, "You boys want out *here*?"

"Yeah," Jake said. "We're, uh, meeting someone."

The driver raised one eyebrow. "Okay, then. You take care, now."

"Thanks," Jake said, hopping onto the sidewalk.

Jake set Cody down and nodded toward the truck stop. "I don't know where we're headed, but I do know it's time for lunch."

"Now you're talkin'!" Taylor exclaimed, his stomach growling.

They hurried over to the truck stop—a sprawling acre of pavement with more than two dozen gas pumps and a large central building. As the boys walked, they passed at least thirty parked trucks, many of them belching out diesel fumes as their drivers attended to business inside the central building.

"You'd better wait outside here with Cody," Jake told Taylor.

"Get me some chips—oh, and some peanut butter cups."

Jake went into the store and quickly began cruising up and down the aisles, filling a plastic basket full of food that would have made a health worker cringe. He grabbed bags of chips and peanut butter cups for Taylor, two large Cokes, and a package of cookies. He returned to the refrigerator and picked out a chunk of cheddar cheese, some baloney, and a quart of milk, then threw in some beef jerky and a large bag of trail mix for good measure. Finally he grabbed two cans of dog food for Cody, along with some doggy treats, and carried the shopping basket to the counter.

That should keep us going for a few days, Jake thought.

A middle-aged woman rang up the food impatiently.

"You want a bag?"

"Yes, please."

With an annoyed grimace, the woman dumped the groceries into two plastic bags. "That'll be $39.72."

Jake handed her a one-hundred-dollar bill from Bull's stash.

Seeing the large denomination, the woman looked at Jake, then back at the bill. She held it up to the light to look for the watermark and security strip, then picked up a special marker and made a dash across the bill. Jake started to get nervous. He tapped his hand on his thigh and looked out the store window with what he hoped was a casual expression.

What's taking her so long?

The cashier hesitated, her hand hovering over the till. "What's a kid like you doing walking around with one-hundred-dollar bills in his pocket?" she asked, fixing Jake with a glare.

"It was, uh, a birthday present," Jake answered, shifting slightly.

The woman ran her eyes up and down Jake's dirty shirt and messed-up hair. "Birthday present, huh? Stolen, more like. Maybe I should call the police, so you can confirm your story with them?"

"What?" Jake blurted. If the police got involved, that was it for him and Taylor. They'd be on the first bus back to Pittsburgh . . . and to Bull. "Don't—that's all I have, I swear!"

"And maybe we'll soon know why," the woman said, reaching for the phone.

9

Acid surged in back of Jake's throat. "Please . . . ," he said, but before he could continue, another voice spoke up behind him.

"Aw, Pam. Cut the kid some slack, will ya?"

Jake turned to see a middle-aged blond woman standing next him. She was dressed in jeans and a trucker's cap. Her arm muscles bulged out of the sleeves of a T-shirt that read KEEP ON TRUCKIN' and had a picture of a speeding truck with flames shooting out the back.

"Oh, it's you, Sharon. I'm just trying to make sure the kid isn't in trouble," the cashier—Pam—responded.

"And if he isn't, you're going to try to make some trouble for him, right?" the truck driver—Sharon—answered. "I swear, since your divorce, you've been more ornery than a rabid possum."

Pam shot her a dirty look. "You stay out of this, Sharon. I got a duty to look out for trouble."

Sharon stepped past Jake. "And maybe I've got a duty to tell other truckers to pass up this choke-and-puke joint and gas up at Roady's Truck Stop two exits back?"

Pam scowled, the gears in her head clicking over. "Fine," she finally said, stuffing the one-hundred-dollar bill into her cash register and slapping Jake's change down on the counter. "But listen, kid, don't let me see you around here again, you hear?"

Jake didn't answer, just scooped up his money and hurried out to where Taylor and Cody waited on a nearby bench.

Taylor grabbed a plastic bag from Jake. "What'd you get?"

"I bought the whole store, but we better not stay here."

"I gotta eat something first," Taylor said, ripping open the bag of chips.

Jake sighed. "All right, but hurry."

Jake popped open two cans of dog food for Cody and set them on the ground. Then he joined Taylor in their junk food feast. Jake was even hungrier than he'd thought. After polishing off half the chunk of cheese, a half bag of chips, and half the carton of milk, he began gnawing on a slice of beef jerky.

"I should have bought more," Jake said.

"So just go back and buy some," Taylor said, his mouth full of cheese and chips.

"Well, I would but—" Jake was about to explain about

the nasty cashier when Sharon, the trucker, walked outside. Spotting the boys and Cody, she walked on over and grinned.

"Every meal's a banquet, huh?"

Jake didn't quite get the joke, but he and Taylor laughed guardedly. "Yeah. Thanks for helping me out in there."

"What do you mean?" Taylor asked. "What happened?"

"Aw, just a little disagreement," Sharon explained. "It was nothing. You boys look like you could use a friend."

Jake didn't respond, so Sharon squatted down to pet Cody. "Cool dog. What's his name?"

"Cody," Taylor answered. "He's the best dog in the universe."

Sharon laughed. "I can see that. Hungry, too."

"We haven't eaten in—" Taylor began, but Jake elbowed him in the ribs.

"Ow! Why'd you—" but then Taylor figured it out.

"Don't worry, fellas," Sharon said, standing back up. "Whatever you've gotten yourselves into, I'm not going to turn you in. I've been on the wrong side of the authorities, and I know that sometimes a person just needs a little help. Speaking of that, is there anything I can do for you kids before I head out?"

Taylor and Jake exchanged glances. They both knew that their options were running low.

"You're a trucker?" Jake asked.

"That I am," Sharon answered. "Drive the finest rig this side of Wall, South Dakota."

"Well," Jake said, "we could use a ride."

Sharon shifted her weight from one leg to the other. "Where you boys headin'?"

Jake was going to make up a location, but Taylor blurted "Wyoming! To see our dad."

Surprise flickered across Sharon's face. "Wyoming? That's a fair piece of highway. Does your mom know where you are—and where you're going?"

Again, before Jake could stop him, Taylor said, "Mom's in the hospital, and Bull—her lousy boyfriend—was gonna come back and mess us up, so we got outta there."

Sharon took a deep breath, concern replacing surprise on her face. Instead of grilling them over more details, though, she asked, "How old are you boys?"

"Sixteen and fifteen," Jake answered, pulling himself up to his full height. He was certainly tall enough, a bean pole like Mrs. Sanchez had said, but it was Taylor who was the giveaway.

Sharon raised an eyebrow. "Sixteen, huh? And short stuff over there?" she asked, switching her gaze to Taylor.

"Hey!" Taylor protested. "I'm not small—I know how to take care of myself. . . ."

Taylor stared back up at Sharon. If anything, the determination in his eyes was the thing that made him look older and wiser than his years. One benefit of living with Bull was that you learned life's hard lessons fast.

A wry smile played at the corners of Sharon's mouth. "And where are you heading in Wyoming?"

"Anywhere will do," Jake said.

Sharon stuck her thumbs into the pockets of her jeans and stared out over the fleet of trucks in the parking area. She remained silent for a few seconds, but then turned her blue eyes back toward the boys.

"Well," she said. "You're in luck. I'm headin' to Reno, Nevada, and I'll be driving across southern Wyoming."

"That's great!" Taylor burst out.

"Yeah, but if my boss finds out I'm givin' rides to runaways, I'm up a creek without a paddle."

"We won't tell anyone—honest!" Taylor said.

Sharon studied them. "No, I don't suppose you will. But understand, I'm only doing this so some creep won't pick you up. Grab your stuff, and let's hit it."

Cody in tow, they walked across the sea of asphalt until they came to a large eighteen-wheeler.

"This is *yours*?" Taylor asked, awestruck.

"Yep. She's a beauty, isn't she?"

Jake was equally impressed. The sheet-metal trailer was nothing special, but the Peterbilt truck cab gleamed turquoise blue with giant chrome exhaust pipes reaching for the sky.

"Can you sleep in there?" Jake asked.

"You bet. Climb in. I'll give you a quick tour."

Taylor lifted Cody into the cab and they climbed up after him. Sharon showed them the cab's bells and whistles, from a spacious bed to a mini-refrigerator, desk, and TV screen.

"Wow! A person could live in here," Taylor said.

Sharon laughed. "Believe me, most times I do. Took me three years to save up for her, but now that she's all bought and paid for, I can start saving for my next project."

"What's that?" Jake asked.

"Aw, tell you later. Time to hit the road. Who wants to ride shotgun?"

"Me!" Taylor shouted, hopping into the front passenger seat. Sharon lowered a little bench seat for Cody to sit on, while Jake sat perched on the bed, which was up a couple of steps from the main cab. From there, he could look out the front, but also out his own side window.

Sharon started up the truck, and Taylor and Jake both watched in amazement as she began shifting through the gears.

"How many gears are there?" Jake asked Sharon as she swung onto Interstate 88 West.

"You can buy 'em with different numbers, but I got a fifteen-speed transmission."

"Fifteen gears!" Taylor exclaimed.

"That's right, and I use every one of 'em. Now shush up for a spell while I make my way out of this traffic."

From the truck stop, Sharon drove west on the interstate, and at first, Chicago never seemed to end. For more than an hour, they passed one shopping center after another. Finally the giant buildings began giving way to farmland, and for the first time in days—maybe weeks—Jake breathed a sigh of relief. Pittsburgh and Bull felt far behind him, and he was driving into the kind of country he'd only read about in books.

Sharon had turned on a country music station on the radio, and she and Taylor carried on an easy conversation in front. Jake let his brother do most of the talking, while he sat, riveted, by the ever-changing landscape.

After another hour Sharon shouted, "Mississippi River coming up!"

"What?" Jake exclaimed, leaning forward.

"You never seen it before?" Sharon called back.

"Not even close," Taylor answered for both of them.

"Well, then, this calls for a celebration!" Sharon reached up and pulled a thin chain hanging from the roof of the cab. The truck's horn blared a series of deep loud blasts.

The boys laughed out loud, but as they rolled onto the wide bridge that separated Illinois from Iowa, they gasped.

"The Mississippi's even bigger than the Ohio River back home!" Taylor exclaimed.

"Look!" Jake pointed. "Is that what I think it is?"

"You betcha!" Sharon answered. "A bald eagle!"

The eagle flew right over the bridge in front of their truck and continued its search for food on up the river.

At Davenport, Iowa, I-88 merged into Interstate 80, which continued straight across the state. By the time they passed through Des Moines, the sun was beginning to sink like an orange fireball on the western horizon. Jake couldn't believe how wide open and flat the country was. Farms spread toward every edge, dotted by barns and silver grain silos.

I'll bet I can see fifty miles in every direction, Jake thought.

It was dark by the time Sharon pulled into a truck stop outside of Omaha for dinner. TRAVELER'S REST flashed in neon green above the building.

"My treat," Sharon told the boys as they made their way into the restaurant and slid into a booth.

A waitress approached with water and menus. "Hey, Sharon. I see you got company tonight."

"Sure do," Sharon answered, giving the waitress a wink. "But let's keep that to ourselves, okay? Don't want their wives to find out."

The boys and the waitress all laughed.

"You already know what you want?" the waitress asked.

"I'd like a—" Taylor began, but Sharon cut him off.

"We're all having the meatloaf special, with plenty of mashed potatoes and green beans. Milk for the boys here, and I'll have coffee."

"Comin' up," the waitress said, flipping her order book closed and walking away.

"Sorry, Taylor," Sharon said. "I couldn't live with myself if you didn't try the meatloaf. It's the best meatloaf this side of Des Moines."

"But the last sign said Des Moines is only a hundred miles away," Taylor objected.

Sharon grinned at him. "You catch on fast."

While they waited for their dinner, Jake asked, "How does that waitress know you? Do you drive through here a lot?"

"At least once a month. I've got friends along the whole interstate highway system."

"It must be cool drivin' a truck," Taylor said.

Sharon's blue eyes seemed to lose focus for a moment, then they snapped back toward the boys. "It's like anything. Got its good and its bad. Sometimes, there's nothin' better than hittin' a wide open highway with plenty of scenery and no one lookin' over your shoulder."

Jake could tell from Sharon's voice that she wasn't telling them the whole story.

"Do you have a family somewhere, or do you drive all the time?" he asked.

Sharon sipped her coffee and slowly spun the cup in its saucer. "Yeah. Two kids. A girl about your age, Jake. A boy two years younger."

"Where are they? Do you ever get to bring them with you?" Taylor asked.

Sharon frowned. "Nope. Fact is, I'm only allowed to see them a couple of times a year, and only with a legal guardian present."

"Whaaaat?" Taylor and Jake looked at each other.

"That's right," Sharon said. "I got my life straight now, but I made some mistakes when I was younger."

"Mistakes?" Jake asked.

"Well," she said. "I don't tell this to too many people, but I got into drugs. Booze, too."

"No way!" Taylor exclaimed. "You?"

Sharon nodded. "Yep. I liked nothing better than to party. But soon I wasn't using the drugs. They were using me, and I tell you, that was a dark road to drive down. I got arrested, thrown in jail."

"No way!" Jake's jaw dropped, revealing a mouthful of half-chewed crackers.

Sharon stared hard at her coffee cup. "Yep. A buncha times. The courts took my kids away and sent me to the state penitentiary for two years. Inside, I kept being a real badass, until I found Jesus and cleaned up my act."

"When did you get out?" Jake asked.

"Five years ago."

"And they still won't give you your kids back?"

"Nope. They live with a foster family. But I'm savin' up for a good lawyer, and soon I'm goin' to try to make us a family again."

Suddenly Jake realized why Sharon had been so kind and helpful to him and Taylor. He'd never thought about what it would be like for a parent missing a child; for him it had always been the other way around.

Sharon wiped moisture from her eyes, and they all sat silently for a moment. Then the waitress appeared with their dinner.

"That's what I'm talkin' about!" Taylor said, picking up his fork.

"Not so fast, young man," Sharon told him. "Just because we're in a truck stop, don't mean we eat like barbarians. Put your napkins in your laps."

Jake and Taylor did as they were told, then Sharon reached across the table with both hands to say a short prayer. The boys glanced at each other, then reached out and linked hands. As they prayed, Jake thought about how far they'd already come, and how grateful he was to have found an adult who would help them instead of getting in their way.

"Now, let's do us some damage to this meatloaf," Sharon said. "We've got a lot of hours to put in on the road tomorrow—and I plan to get started nice and early!"

10

Sharon wasn't kidding.

That night she booked the boys a motel room outside of North Platte, Nebraska, while she slept in her truck. Jake felt like his head had barely hit the pillow when he heard a loud knocking on the motel room door. He sat straight up, heart pounding. For a sickening moment he thought he was back in Pittsburgh and that Bull was trying to break down the door. Then he recognized the motel room and hurried to the door, Cody at his heels.

"Who is it?" he muttered.

"It's me, Jake."

He opened the door to see Sharon smiling, holding a cup of coffee. She wore a fresh T-shirt that read A BAD

ATTITUDE IS LIKE A FLAT TIRE. YOU CAN'T GO ANYWHERE UNTIL YOU CHANGE IT.

Jake couldn't help but smile.

"Time to crank up your engines, boys," Sharon said. "We got a lot of road to reel in. Meet me at the truck in fifteen minutes."

Jake had to splash water on Taylor to wake him up, but the boys went to the bathroom, got dressed, and staggered out to find Sharon checking over the tires on the eighteen-wheeler. The three of them jumped into the cab and pulled back onto the interstate just as golden streaks of dawn were creeping over the horizon. The boys scarfed down a couple of yogurts each, along with some bagels and cheese that they found in Sharon's mini-fridge.

"Will we make it to Wyoming today?" Taylor asked Sharon.

"Ought to be there in a couple of hours."

Taylor spun around. "Did you hear that, Jake? We'll be in the Tetons in two hours!"

"Whoa, cowboy! I didn't say that," said Sharon. "I said we'll be in *Wyoming* in two hours. Wyoming's a big state. If you're goin' to the Tetons, I think the best place to let you off is Rock Springs. From there, you gotta head north."

"How much farther is it?" Jake asked.

"About another three hours."

Sharon shifted into a higher gear. "I wish I could take you myself, but I'm already runnin' late with this load. If I don't get it to Reno on time, I won't get paid."

BRANDON WALLACE

84

"That's okay," Jake said. "We'll figure out something."

While Sharon drove and chatted with Taylor, Jake pulled out his father's journal and letter, scouring them for clues. He studied the map with the sketch of the lake with the waterfall coming down into it—or near it, he couldn't decide which.

Look across the moose's neck, he read again. What did that mean?

Jake shook his head, and for the first time he wondered if they'd made the right decision leaving Pittsburgh.

It's crazy trying to look for Dad, he thought. *How are we going to find him in millions of acres of wilderness? And what about Mom? Maybe we should have stayed with her. Bull might have left us alone; maybe social services wouldn't have separated us.*

But Jake didn't really believe any of that—he couldn't be sure that he and Taylor weren't in danger while Bull was around. The only person who could help them now was their father.

What if we can't find him? What if we do find him? What would I even say? Would I even recognize him? Will we make it before the police stop us and things get complicated?

A loud voice brought him back to consciousness.

"Wake up, sleepyheads!" Sharon said. "We're here. Rock Springs."

"Huh? Already?" Jake sat up from the truck's bed and looked out the window to see yet another truck stop, with a town and mountains beyond that. He glanced at Taylor, who had fallen asleep in the front passenger seat and was now yawning and rubbing his eyes.

"Make sure you get all your stuff," Jake told his brother.

Taylor stepped up to the truck's "living room," and the boys double-checked that nothing had fallen from their backpacks. Then they and Cody hopped out of the truck.

Sharon walked around to meet them by the truck's front grill.

"Well," Jake told Sharon. "Thank you for the ride."

"And everything else," Taylor added. "It was cool riding in your truck."

Jake couldn't imagine how else they would have come so far in so short a time—riding in the truck was a thousand times better than the dirty and cold freight train.

"To tell you the truth, I enjoyed the company," Sharon said, but her face was scrunched up in concern.

"What's wrong?" Jake asked her.

Sharon hesitated, then said, "Listen, boys. I've been thinking about this, and the more I think about it, the more I just don't feel right about you headin' up to look for your dad all by yourselves—even if you do have a trusty guard dog with you."

Jake glanced down at Cody, who was wagging his tail, ready for action, but then Jake returned his gaze to Sharon.

"Your mama must be worried sick about you," Sharon continued. "And if you're really worried about her boyfriend—what's his name, Bull?—well, I'm thinkin' you can ride out to Reno with me, and we can get in touch with social services."

"No!" Jake blurted, alarmed. He'd thought Sharon was on their side, and now she was talking about getting the authorities involved. "C'mon, Taylor, we'd better go."

Taylor looked uncertainly between Sharon and Jake.

"Now, don't get all torqued out of shape," Sharon told them. "It was just an idea. You might look older, but I know you kids aren't sixteen."

"Yes, we *are*." Jake tried to control the quaver in his voice. He knew Sharon was just trying to look out for them, but he couldn't let anyone else get involved. They had to find their dad for themselves.

"My point is that there are a lot of bad people out there—people who will try to take advantage of two boys on the run, no matter how old you are. I'd like to help you out if I can."

"Thank you. You really helped us a lot. We mean it, but . . . But we can take care of ourselves."

Sharon didn't give up. "Jake. Taylor. I'd want someone helping you if you were my kids and on the run."

"We don't need any more help," Jake repeated more forcefully. "C'mon, Taylor," he said, grabbing his brother's arm. "Let's get out of here."

The boys and Cody quickly headed for the truck stop, Taylor calling a quick good-bye over his shoulder.

"Jake, Taylor," Sharon called after them. "Can't we at least talk about this?"

Sharon took several steps after them, but she stopped when Jake shot her a fearful glance over his shoulder.

"C'mon, hurry," he told Taylor. "We can't stick around here."

"You think Sharon's gonna call the cops?"

"I don't know—and I don't want to find out."

Carrying Cody under his shirt, Jake led Taylor into the truck stop, and they ducked inside the restroom. As Jake washed up, he looked at himself and his brother in the bathroom mirror. They'd showered at the motel the night before, but their clothes were filthy.

Man, no one's going to give us a ride looking this way.

"What are we going to do now, Jake?"

"I don't—"

Just then the bathroom door swung open, and four men filed into the restroom.

Jake's heart skipped a beat, thinking Sharon might have sent the men in to get them. Then he saw that the men all wore similar shorts and Hawaiian-style shirts, with sunglasses hanging around their necks or tucked into their shirt pockets.

Tourists! Jake thought to himself—and that gave him an idea.

"Follow me," he whispered to Taylor.

The tourists gave the boys and Cody curious glances

as they headed for the bathroom door. Looking out into the truck stop store, the boys paused to make sure Sharon wasn't waiting for them.

"All clear," Jake murmured.

Back outside, the boys stopped again while Jake surveyed the parking lot.

"What are you looking for?" Taylor asked him.

Suddenly Jake grinned. "There!" He said with a flick of his head.

Taylor followed Jake's gaze to a bus parked across the lot. Coaches were lined up from all across the country, with different destinations posted in the windows. Jake scanned them until he found the one he was after, and then he pointed it out to Taylor.

"The sign on the front," Taylor exclaimed. "It's going to the Grand Tetons!"

The coach was a tour bus, and the last of the passengers were getting off to stretch their legs

"We gotta get on that bus," Taylor hissed. "It'll take us right to the park!"

Jake's heart thundered again, but his grin faltered.

"They're never going to let us on like this," he told Taylor. "Look at our clothes."

"Maybe we can buy tickets," Taylor said

"Or maybe we don't need tickets. . . . I've got an idea."

Jake led Taylor and Cody away from the bus.

"Where are we going?" Taylor asked.

"Shh. You'll see."

The boys and Cody walked past some of the eighteen-wheelers, and then circled around behind the coach. Crouching behind a truck's rear trailer, Jake spied on the bus. All the passengers appeared to have left to go into the truck stop, but he didn't know if the driver was still on board. Then he saw a man in a gray uniform talking on a cell phone step off and wander toward the building.

"C'mon. Quick!" Jake said.

The boys ran up to the side of the bus, and Jake lifted the latch on one of the big luggage compartments above the undercarriage. The first compartment was locked, but the second one opened with a squeal.

"We're going to get in *there*?" Taylor asked.

"Sharon said it's only three hours up to the Tetons," Jake said. "We ought to be okay."

"What if we get trapped?" Taylor asked.

"We won't!" Jake said impatiently. "Now, get in!"

Looking doubtful, Taylor climbed in over a couple of suit-cases to an empty space at the back of the compartment.

"Cody, come!" Taylor called, and the terrier hopped in after him.

Jake tossed his backpack to Taylor and crawled in on top of a duffel bag. With a last glance to make sure no one had seen them, he reached up and pulled down hard on the edge of the compartment door. It slammed shut, plunging them into darkness.

The enclosed pitch-black space sent a shiver of fear through Jake—it couldn't be more different from Sharon's truck. The heavy diesel motor hummed, and the bus rumbled around them as it moved, jolting them up and down in the darkness.

"Get the flashlight out of your pack," Jake said.

Jake heard Taylor rummaging around, and a moment later a dim yellowish light filled the compartment. The boys were on their way to the Grand Tetons, but it wasn't exactly comfortable; not only was it dark, the luggage compartment soon became like a hot and sweaty sauna.

"I'm thirsty," Taylor said.

"Me too," Jake told him. "Did you refill your water bottle?"

"No . . ."

"Me neither."

First Rule, Jake scolded himself. *Always make sure our water bottles are filled.*

"We'll have to find something in this luggage," Jake said.

Jake knew that stealing was wrong, but right now he didn't see that they had much choice. Already, sweat beaded up on his forehead, and he was feeling sick to his stomach. He imagined that Taylor felt the same way.

The boys began opening the bags around them. In one suitcase, Jake found a map of Wyoming and stuffed it into his pack, but what they really needed now was water, and maybe some food.

"Nothing here," Taylor said, closing up a large plastic suitcase, grabbing on to it to regain his balance. It was so hot and stuffy, he was starting to feel dizzy.

"Not here, either," Jake said, moving on to another bag, when suddenly Taylor let out a cry.

"Score!" Taylor whooped.

Jake glanced over to see his brother pulling four granola bars and a bag of trail mix from a large blue-and-black backpack.

Jake grinned. "Nice."

Then Taylor's grin became even wider as he pulled out two unopened plastic bottles of water. "Jackpot!"

The boys twisted off the caps of the bottles and began guzzling down the water like they were in the desert. Taylor tore open a granola bar. "You want one, Jake?"

"Uh, maybe later." The water helped, but Jake still felt queasy as the coach bumped and jerked along the road.

The ride seemed to last forever, and the longer it lasted, the more worried the boys grew. Taylor's questions just added to Jake's growing anxiety.

"Jake, what if the sign on the bus was wrong? What if this bus isn't going to the Tetons at all? Maybe it just *came* from the Tetons, and we end up in Mexico or something?"

"Taylor, this bus is *not* going to Mexico."

"But what if it is? Then, when we drive through the desert, we'll be boiled alive! And what if we run out of air in here before the bus stops?"

"Taylor—" Jake was getting exasperated, but before he could continue, the bus began to slow.

"What's happening?" Taylor asked.

"We must be stopping. See, I told you we weren't going to Mexico!" Jake laughed. Taylor just rolled his eyes and zipped up his backpack as the giant vehicle jerked to a halt with a loud hiss.

"Where are we?" Taylor whispered.

"I'm not sure, but wherever it is, we need to make a quick exit—the driver isn't going to be happy when he opens that door!" Jake replied.

The boys grabbed their packs and prepared to move as they heard footsteps overhead. Crouched and ready, they heard muffled voices outside, then suddenly a creaking swoosh as the luggage compartment door flew up and open. The boys gulped in the fresh air and shielded their eyes against the bright light. Cody barked and leaped out of the bus.

"What the—?" a man exclaimed. The bus driver and several startled passengers stood staring at them.

Jake and Taylor didn't hang around to explain. "Thanks for the ride, mister!" Taylor said with a grin. "Are we in the Tetons?"

The driver found his voice and demanded, "Yes, we're in the Tetons, and who are you? What were you doing in there?"

"Sorry, can't stop!" Jake whooped, jumping down from

the bus and pushing through the startled passengers. The boys sprinted away, the driver making a feeble attempt to stop them.

"Hey, you kids! Get back here!" he shouted.

But the boys ignored the shouts. Across the parking lot, Jake spotted a road and a line of trees behind it. *This is our shot.*

"This way, Taylor. Go!"

11

Jake finally slowed and came to a halt, his chest heaving. "Wait, Taylor. I don't think they followed us. I think we can stop running!"

They glanced behind them but saw no sign of the bus driver through the trees. Cody, who had dashed ahead, stopped and came trotting back. He cocked his head as if to say, *Why'd you stop? That was fun!*

"You see the look on that guy's face?" Taylor asked Jake, laughing.

"Yeah! He looked like he'd seen a ghost—or two!"

The boys emerged out of the patch of aspen trees and into a sun-splashed green meadow. Sage- and grass-covered hills rose in front of them. Behind that towered the spectacular snow-glazed peaks of the Grand Tetons themselves.

"Wow!" exclaimed Taylor. "Jake, you ever seen mountains like those?"

Jake took a deep breath of sage-scented air and studied the peaks. They seemed impossibly jagged and tall. "Only in books," he replied, taking it all in.

Right then both boys smelled campfire smoke. Taylor's stomach rumbled. "Oh, man. I smell something good cookin'. Let's go find where it's coming from."

Taylor started in the direction of the smells, but his brother stopped him. "We gotta stay out of sight. You don't want someone to report us and send us back to Bull, do you?"

Fear flashed across Taylor's face, and Jake regretted bringing up their mom's boyfriend. "Come here," he told his brother. "Let's figure out where we are."

They plunked down on a nearby rock. Jake took out their father's letter while Taylor spread out the map of Wyoming that they'd found in the bus compartment. Most of the map didn't show enough detail to really help them, but Taylor located a close-up insert of Grand Teton and Yellowstone National Parks.

Jake said, "Dad writes here something about seeing the aurora borealis, and leaving inspiration behind us."

"Huh? What's inspiration?" Taylor asked. "What's the aurora borealis?"

"Well," Jake said, waffling, "inspiration is something that, you know, *inspires* you."

"You mean, like, when you sweat?"

Despite being hungry and tired, Jake laughed. "No, that's *perspire*."

Taylor laughed too.

"Inspire is when something makes you feel good about yourself," Jake explained. "It makes you want to do better."

"Or be better."

Jake nodded. "Yeah. But I don't know what aurora borealis is. It sounds familiar, but . . ."

"What else does the letter say?" Taylor asked.

"Well, there's that thing about looking across the moose's neck, but nothing that tells us which way to go."

"Look," Taylor said, pointing to their new map. "Here's something called Inspiration Point next to Jenny Lake. You think that's what he meant when he said leaving inspiration behind?"

Jake followed Taylor's finger, and his heart beat faster. "That could be it. Let's head toward it. It looks like it's north of us on the map. You got the compass?"

Taylor pulled the instrument from his pocket. Both boys knew how to use it from summer camp the previous year, and Taylor quickly located the right direction. "That way."

"Okay, let's get farther away from the road, and then we can head north."

Cody didn't need to be told twice. He dashed through the sagebrush, and the boys set out after him.

They followed animal trails—the boys weren't sure

what kind—north and west for about a mile. After fifteen minutes they surprised a jackrabbit, standing tall, nose quivering, staring at them.

"Jake!" Taylor shouted, but as soon as the word left his mouth, the rabbit spooked and bounded away on its long powerful legs. Cody tore after him.

"Bring us some dinner, Cody!" Taylor yelled, but moments later the dog reappeared—without the rabbit in his mouth.

"Well, I guess we know what's making these trails through the brush." Jake laughed.

Half a mile farther, they intersected one of the park's hiking trails. They turned right and followed it north to Taggart Lake. Although the Tetons rose steeply only a mile or two to their left, the trail undulated up and down through the hilly sage country. Sometimes it veered through lodgepole pines or aspen groves, but then it returned to the sagebrush, and before long the boys spotted a group of hikers getting closer to them.

Jake's eyes quickly sought a hiding place, but the sagebrush offered nothing.

"What should we do?" Taylor hissed.

"Just act natural, and let me do the talking," Jake told him.

Cody ran ahead to greet the hikers, a man and a woman carrying heavy day packs. The woman stopped to pet Cody as Jake and Taylor walked up to them.

"Sorry about that," Jake said. "He likes people."

"So cute!" the woman crooned. Cody basked in the attention.

"How are you guys?" the man asked. The couple looked like they could be college students, or maybe a bit older.

"Pretty good," Jake responded. "How about you?" He didn't want to get into a long conversation, but he figured he had to ask.

"We're great," said the man. Waving at the towering Teton peaks, he then asked, "Who wouldn't be great on a day like this? It's your first time here?"

"Uh, yeah," Jake said.

"Us too."

"This is the prettiest spot we've ever been," the woman added, standing straight again. "Are you here alone?"

Jake and Taylor quickly glanced at each other.

"Oh, uh, our parents are waiting for us at the end of the trail."

The man nodded. "Well, be careful. The rangers said they've seen grizzlies around here."

"Really?" Taylor asked, fear edging his excitement.

"That's what they said. You have bear spray?"

"Right in my pack," Jake lied.

"Well, you might want to carry it on your belt," said the man. "If you see a bear, you won't have time to pull it out."

"Okay. Thanks."

The boys said good-bye to the couple and continued hiking. When they were out of earshot, Jake sighed heavily.

"Man, I didn't like that. They asked a lot of questions."

"And what's with the bears?" Taylor asked, a note of fear edging his voice. "I don't like the sound of *that*!"

"We have to be extra careful now that we're out in the wild," Jake said. "There are worse wild animals than Bull out here!"

As they approached Bradley Lake, the boys decided to delve into their precious food supply. Jake chose a can of tuna fish, but by the time they shared it with Cody, they only felt hungrier. Searching through his pack, Jake discovered an even worse problem.

"Uh-oh."

"What?" Taylor asked.

"I think I'm out of water," Jake replied.

"That's okay. We can share," Taylor said, handing Jake his own water bottle.

Jake smiled at his brother. "Thanks, but that's not gonna last very long."

Taylor laughed and pointed to Bradley Lake. "But there's water all over the place here."

"Yeah, but it's probably dirty—we don't wanna catch something!"

Taylor nodded. "What can we do, then? I don't see any drinking fountains around here."

"Well," Jake said. "You remember at camp, they told us we should boil water to make it safe. Or put those little pills in it, or filter it."

"We don't have any pills or a filter, do we?"

Jake shook his head.

"Well, then we can boil it when we make camp."

Jake nodded. "Yeah. Until then, we're going to have to ration our supply."

"No problem," said Taylor. "I'm part camel."

"In that case, you can give me a ride!" Jake said, pretending to hop up onto Taylor.

The boys continued their trek to Bradley Lake, where the trail forked. One path led up into the mountains, and Jake longed to follow it, but he knew they weren't ready to go so far off track. Besides, that trail would lead them away from their destination, Jenny Lake. Instead the boys turned right, down through more sagebrush and grass meadows.

A riot of wildflowers soon surrounded them. Jake recognized many of the flowers from his father's journal: the lavender-and-white blooms of lupine; the sun-splashed yellow flowers of arrowleaf balsamroot; purple shooting stars and larkspur and many more.

"It's so colorful here," exclaimed Taylor. "Nothin' like our place in Pennsylvania."

"Yeah, I can see why Dad wanted to come out here."

"I wish I remembered Dad better," Taylor said. "What do you think he'll be like?"

"I don't remember a whole lot myself," Jake admitted. "He was big and had a long brown beard. He used to take us walking through the Pennsylvania woods all the time, looking for birds and mushrooms. He'd just toss you up on his shoulders and off we'd go."

"Was he nice? Nicer than Bull?"

Jake snorted. "A crocodile's nicer than Bull."

"Seriously, Jake."

"He was nice. You'll like him."

Jake didn't tell him about the fights he remembered. How his mother and father yelled at each other about work and money and their father's plans to move out West. He also didn't tell Taylor about the day their dad finally left. The day that had broken Jake's heart forever.

"Hey, look!" Taylor shouted, interrupting Jake's thoughts.

In the distance, maybe half a mile a way, a group of enormous brown rocks seemed to be sitting in a field. As Jake watched, one of the rocks began to move.

"Bison!" Jake shouted.

"Awesome!" Taylor yelled.

Cody couldn't tell what the boys were looking at, but he caught their excitement. He yipped and pranced around like a circus animal.

Jake and Taylor cracked up.

"It's a good thing they aren't any closer," Taylor said. "Cody would start a stampede. Did you ever think we'd be seeing *real live bison*?"

Jake shook his head. "Never even crossed my mind. Look at them! They're something, aren't they?"

Amazed, the boys stood and watched the large mammals grazing.

"C'mon," Jake said. "Let's keep going. Maybe we can get a better view of them."

They brushed through the long grass, Taylor leading the way, laughing as they approached the huge animals that loomed in the distance. But as they got closer to a small running stream, Taylor suddenly froze and gasped.

Jake almost collided with him. "Hey! What gives?"

His hand trembling, Taylor pointed at the ground. Jake's eyes widened as he saw what had freaked Taylor out. There, in the middle of the trail, angry and menacing, was a snake. It was hissing and ready to strike!

12

The snake's jaws were wide open, exposing the red flesh of its mouth. Two-thirds of the serpent's body lay coiled like a spring, ready to launch an attack. Suddenly Cody barked and moved toward the snake, snapping the boys into action.

Taylor seized the dog by the scruff and dragged him away. "Cody, get back!"

Jake also leaped back—almost tripping over a sage bush. When he straightened up, though, he peered at the snake more closely. After a moment he stepped closer.

"Jake, what are you *doing*?" Taylor yelled.

"Can you see its pupils?" Jake asked, peering at the snake.

"No, and I don't want to!" Taylor shouted.

The snake hissed again, and Jake moved almost to

within striking distance. The markings of the snake looked familiar, like something he'd read about in his dad's journal.

"Its pupils are round," he told his brother. "There's only one snake in the United States that has round pupils *and* is venomous. The coral snake. And this doesn't look anything like a coral snake."

"I don't care. That thing looks like it wants to kill us!"

Right on cue, the snake struck at Jake. The full length of its body uncoiled and launched itself toward him. Jake jerked back out of harm's way, his heart racing.

"Whoa! That was close!" said Taylor.

"I think it's just scared," Jake said, unslinging his backpack. As Taylor and Cody backed away, Jake pulled out their dad's journal and began looking for the sketch he'd seen.

"Here," he said. Reluctantly, Taylor moved closer. Jake pointed to a pencil drawing his father had made of a skinny serpent with stripes on it.

"This looks like the same snake, doesn't it?" Jake asked his brother.

Taylor—still clutching Cody—looked from the drawing to the snake and back again. "I guess . . . ?"

"Well, it says here that it's a garter snake—'a harmless species common to this part of the state.'"

"Did you say harmless?"

"Right. Look how tiny its teeth are. It could bite you, and you probably wouldn't even feel it."

"No, thanks," Taylor said, but his body relaxed.

"Keep Cody back," Jake said, and with his shoe, he nudged the snake off the trail. The garter snake hissed again but didn't strike. Instead it quickly slithered into the grass and disappeared under a nearby rock. When the snake had gone, Taylor and Jake stared at each other. Then they both burst out laughing.

"Boy, do we have a lot to learn," said Taylor.

Jake nodded, but his thoughts turned serious, remembering the hikers' warning about grizzly bears—they might not be so lucky the next time they met a wild animal. It wasn't just the likes of Bull and the authorities that were out to get them. Here, there were wild animals to be avoided. Their lives could actually be in danger.

"We should try to pick up some of that bear spray somewhere."

"Cody'll protect us," Taylor said. The terrier was busily sniffing the rock the garter snake had disappeared under.

"Maybe," Jake said, not sounding too sure.

Still amped from their "near-death" encounter with the snake, Jake, Taylor, and Cody hopped the stream and continued along the trail. By now, the bison had wandered out of sight, but the boys soon had bigger concerns than bison. Even though the afternoon sun had dipped behind the mountain peaks, the dry warm air had forced them to drink the last of Taylor's water.

"Man, it's hot," Taylor complained as they staggered up another low-rising hill.

"Yeah," Jake agreed, salty sweat stinging his eyes. For the hundredth time he kicked himself for forgetting to fill his water bottle. He couldn't remember ever feeling this thirsty, and Taylor was barely managing to stagger along behind him on the trail. Even Cody's long pink tongue hung out.

Taylor halted and bent over, hands on his knees. "Jake, I don't feel so good."

"What's wrong?" Jake walked back to his brother and squatted down to look him in the eyes.

"My muscles keep knotting up, and my stomach . . ."

"You feel like you're going to throw up?"

Taylor breathed heavily. "Maybe."

Jake straightened back up—now he was seriously worried. His own calf muscles were cramping, and his skin felt a lot hotter than it should. They had already come dangerously close to running out of water on the bus. But here they weren't going to stumble across any bottled water.

We need to find water, fast.

Jake pulled out their map. He saw that a large lake lay about a mile ahead, but he didn't know if Taylor could make it that far.

On second thought, I might not be able to make it a mile either.

Just then he heard a noise overhead and swiveled to see a couple of ducks flying less than fifty feet over their heads. They looked like they were coming in for a landing somewhere.

"C'mon," Jake told his brother. "There might be some water through those trees."

Taylor didn't speak, just forced himself to follow his brother. Jake led them through a hundred yards of sagebrush. Cody seemed to sense something up ahead and ran in front of them, following another rabbit trail until they reached some cottonwood trees. It was only a half mile to where the birds had landed, and Jake wanted to urge his brother on, but his tongue was sticking to the roof of his mouth. Instead he just nodded. He could see dark rings forming around Taylor's green eyes and wondered if his brother could go on. But the younger boy brushed back the hair from his sweating forehead, and soldiered on under the blazing sun.

Through the trees, hidden from the trail, the trio finally emerged into the clearing where the birds had landed. Cattails grew on the side of a small pond, and two ducks—*mallards,* Jake thought—paused in their feeding to warily eye the intruders. Jake felt like kissing the ground in relief as he saw the bright sunlight bounce back off the water's shimmering surface.

"Water!" Taylor shouted. He dropped his pack, and without even undressing, he plunged into the pool. Panicked, the ducks took off, but Cody sprinted after Taylor and also leaped in.

Taylor gulped huge mouthfuls of the water. Jake could only hope that if it was good enough for the birds, it was good enough for them. He also dropped his pack and then dove into the pool.

"It's freezing!" he shouted.

"I know! Isn't it great?" Taylor asked. He swam on his back like an otter, Cody happily paddling along behind him.

"Don't drink too much of it, Taylor," Jake warned again. "Remember, we need to boil it first."

"It tastes fine," Taylor said, taking another drink.

"Yeah, but it's not how it tastes . . . ," Jake began, but then he, too, surrendered and took a huge swallow himself.

The boys stayed in the pond until the cold stabbed needles through their flesh. Smiling, they finally staggered out and flopped down on the bank.

"Man, that felt good," said Taylor.

"You can say that again."

"Man, that felt good."

Jake threw a stick at him. Already, both the boys felt better, and Taylor was back to his normal goofy self.

"This is a great spot," said Taylor. "Maybe we should stay here tonight."

Jake surveyed the pond and its surroundings. It actually did seem like a good place to camp. The trees kept them hidden from other hikers and nosey rangers. Beneath the trees and in the surrounding brush, there were plenty of dead sticks and logs that they could use to build a fire.

"Okay," said Jake, "but it's going to get cold early. Let's wash our clothes and get them hung up to dry."

Taylor groaned, but the swim in the pond had revived him.

"You rinse them out," Jake told him. "Even the ones we're wearing."

"*What?*" Taylor stared, his mouth open. "You want us to walk around naked?"

Jake sighed and waved his arm at their surroundings. "Taylor, who's going to see us out here?"

Taylor glanced around. "Those ducks might come back!"

Jake couldn't help laughing. He stepped out of his underwear and threw his boxers at his brother. "Just do it."

"Oh, great," Taylor grumbled. "Now I have to wash your stinky old underwear." He gathered all their clothes together, though, and got started.

While Taylor did laundry, Jake started thinking about a fire. He pulled his dad's journal out from his pack to see what he could find.

The journal sketch showed twigs leaned up against a log or a rock, with larger and larger sticks crossed back and forth over it, forming a crude lean-to grating. Another note said, *Put paper under here*, and had an arrow pointing under the grating.

As Taylor hung up their dripping clothes on the low branches of some young cottonwood trees, Jake gathered sticks of different size and thickness. Then he carefully arranged the sticks against a medium-size dead cottonwood log. He couldn't find any paper to use as a starter, but he did find plenty of dried dead cottonwood leaves.

"These will probably burn," he muttered to himself.

Taylor finished hanging the clothes and walked over. Already, both boys had forgotten they were naked.

"What are you doing?" Taylor asked.

"Just getting a fire ready," said Jake. "Go get the matches, okay?"

"Sure, where are they?"

Jake looked at him. "Very funny. They're in your pack."

Taylor shook his head. "I didn't pack any matches. Did you?"

Jake groaned. "Are you serious? I just thought . . ."

"What?"

"Never mind."

"Maybe we can rub some sticks together," Taylor suggested. "Or use an ax like that boy did in *Hatchet*?"

"We don't have an ax."

"We've got pocketknives."

Jake shrugged. "It's worth a try."

He dug out his pocketknife, and then found a couple of different kinds of rocks. He whacked the blade of the knife against the rocks, but nothing happened.

"Here, let me try," said Taylor, trying to coax some sparks out of the knife.

"All we're doing is messing up the blade," Jake finally said.

"Let's try sticks."

Jake was pretty sure that wasn't going to work either, but he said, "Be my guest."

By this time, chilly air had begun to flow down from the snow-covered peaks. Fortunately, their clothes had almost dried, so the boys got dressed again. Jake took out a can of spaghetti with sauce and opened it.

"Any luck with the fire?" Jake called.

Taylor threw the sticks down in disgust. "Can't even get them warm," he said, and wandered back over to Jake.

"Well, dinner is served."

The two brothers sat on the ground, passing the can of cold spaghetti back and forth, sharing some with Cody. They were still so hungry, they decided to open another can, and they quickly devoured that, too.

"Man, I could eat ten of those things," said Taylor as the last light began fading above the mountains.

"Me too. What do you say we eat the last of our peanut butter cups?"

Taylor's face brightened. "Sure! I forgot we had any of those left!"

When unwrapped, the candy looked like little balls of moose poop after being melted and cooled over and over, but Jake and Taylor didn't mind.

"Man, this is the best dessert I've ever eaten," Taylor exclaimed.

"Yeah," Jake muttered.

As they were licking their fingers, another gust of cool wind made Jake ponder the night ahead.

"It's almost dark. We need to make a bed of some kind."

"What about using leaves, like Dad showed in his journal?"

Jake nodded. Together the boys dug a shallow depression under a nearby tree. They lined it with leaves and then piled another mound of leaves next to it. By the time they finished, the temperature had begun to drop dramatically, and they put on every piece of clothing they had in their packs.

Then both boys sat down in their bed of leaves and piled the extra leaves on top of them. Cody snuggled between them, carving out a place for himself in the makeshift bed. Using their packs for pillows, they stared up through the cottonwood branches to watch the stars pop out of the sky one by one.

"This isn't so bad." Jake sighed.

"These leaves are a little scratchy, but it beats being back in Pittsburgh with Bull, that's for sure," Taylor agreed.

With mostly full stomachs and each other and Cody to keep them warm, the boys listened to the croaking of frogs and the hoot of an owl. For the first time since leaving Pittsburgh, Jake relaxed enough to appreciate the sense of adventure coursing through him. For the first time in weeks, he fell asleep with a smile on his lips.

13

Their nest kept them warm—for a while.

After a couple of hours Jake woke up shivering. He scooted closer to Taylor and Cody, who also squirmed to keep warm, but whichever position he tried would leave his other side more exposed to the cold air. When pale light finally brightened the eastern horizon, a new problem swarmed in—mosquitoes. Even with the hood of his parka pulled tightly around his head, the pesky insects managed to find bare skin, and in no time Jake could feel at least a dozen bites swelling around his cheeks and neck.

After swatting away the buzzing bloodsuckers and trying to get warm, Jake finally raised the surrender flag and crawled out of their leaf-filled bed. Cody just stared at him as he stood up, content to stay snuggled against Taylor.

"Man's best friend, my foot," Jake grumbled at him.

After taking a drink of water, Jake explored the lakeshore. The mosquitoes continued to follow him, and he wished he'd thought to throw some insect repellent into his pack before they left. He remembered a trick he and Taylor had learned at summer camp last year—rubbing mud over exposed areas of skin. *Maybe we could try that later,* he thought. *What we really need is a good shelter.*

The leaf bed was better than the floor of the freight car on their ride out to Chicago, but not by much. As he walked along the shore, though, he suddenly stopped. About a hundred yards away, a mound of sticks and mud rose up out of the water. It was about the size of one of those tents they used on mountain-climbing expeditions, and even though he'd never seen one of these stick structures with his own eyes, Jake immediately recognized it.

"A beaver lodge!" he exclaimed.

Jake sat down on the shore, hoping to see a beaver pop his head out. Unfortunately, the beavers stayed out of sight, but Jake did enjoy watching a pair of redheaded ducks with sharp pointed bills paddle around the lake with their babies trailing behind. Sitting quietly, he also saw the eyes of a frog pop up from some waterweeds near the shoreline, and a very fast bird with swept-back wings dart over the lake.

I'll bet that's some kind of falcon, Jake thought to himself, *looking for a meal.*

Just the thought of food sent Jake's stomach growling, and soon he stood up and hurried back to camp. He found Taylor and Cody rummaging through their packs.

"Any food left?" Jake asked.

"That's what I'm looking for," Taylor said. "There's some cheese, but I think it's gone bad."

"Any chips left?"

Taylor gave him a look. "Like we'd leave those lying around. All I found is a couple of packs of Pop-Tarts."

He held out one to Jake, and they sat down to breakfast. Each package held two cinnamon-flavored pastries, and the boys inhaled the first one faster than you could say *gulp*.

"Every meal's a banquet," Taylor said.

Jake looked over at him, and they laughed. But Jake felt a twinge of guilt, thinking about Sharon.

"I feel bad running off like that," Jake admitted, giving half of his second Pop-Tart to Cody. "She did a lot for us."

Taylor did the same, then said, "Maybe after we find Dad, we can send her something to the Traveler's Rest—she does spend a lotta time there."

"Like what?"

"I don't know. A present. She seems to like T-shirts."

"Good idea," said Jake. "But first we gotta figure out what we're going to do today."

"This lake's pretty nice. Do you think we should stay here?"

Jake shook his head. "Too many mosquitoes, and besides, the sooner we find Dad, the better."

"Man, I'm hungry."

"Yeah, me too. I never thought I'd miss the sloppy joes at school."

Taylor chuckled. "Maybe we can catch some fish. Do you think there's any in this lake?"

"Yeah, a few, but I think we should keep going. Dad said to leave inspiration behind, right? From the map, Inspiration Point's only a couple of miles away. Maybe we'll find another clue there—and a better campsite."

Taylor swatted at a cloud of mosquitoes buzzing around his face. "Well, what are we waiting for?"

The boys quickly packed up what little gear they had, and set off. Even though the sun now crawled above the horizon, Jake figured it was only about seven in the morning, and the boys and Cody had the trail to themselves. In no time they'd covered the distance to the south end of Jenny Lake, and they paused on the shoreline to look at their map.

"It says there's a visitor center right over there," Taylor said, pointing to the east side of the lake. "Maybe we could get some food there. And a better map of the park."

Jake frowned. "Yeah, but what if people are looking for us?"

"Well, we can do what we did before," said Taylor. "I can stay hidden with Cody while you go in to check it out."

Jake knew it was risky—but so was starving to death or getting lost in the wilderness.

"Okay," he said. "Let's do it." He spit in his hands and rubbed the dirt off his face in an effort to look a little less disheveled. He wasn't sure how well it worked.

The Jenny Lake Visitor Center lay about half a mile away and was just opening up when Jake walked in, trying to look like a regular tourist. He casually picked up one of the park service maps and opened it. It was a lot better than what they had, but he was hoping for something else he'd learned about at camp last year.

"May I help you?" asked a man in his forties or so, wearing a wide-brimmed ranger hat and a gold tag that read PETE GARCIA.

"Um, yeah," said Jake. "My, uh, parents sent me in to see if you have, um, any topographical maps of the area."

"You planning to head into the backcountry?" Ranger Garcia asked.

"Um, not this trip, but maybe next year or something."

The ranger smiled. "Glad to hear it. Too many people just race through the park in their RVs and cars, and don't take time to explore."

Jake smiled back at him. "Well, I wish we had time this year."

The ranger went to a little cabinet and pulled out a large map and laid it out in front of Jake. "This is the largest scale we have," said Ranger Garcia. "It should give you enough detail. . . ." He paused, glancing sidelong at Jake, as if remembering something. Shaking his head, forgetting again, he continued, "Erm, but if you want even more, you might try the forest service office down in Jackson Hole."

"This is great, thanks," Jake said, looking at the ranger suspiciously.

That was weird, he thought as he hit the restroom, pausing to take a long drink from the faucet and then refilling the water bottles. But as he made his way back down the corridor, he suddenly understood, and a feeling of dread filled his stomach. Pinned to the corner of the bulletin board, he saw a sign that made his heart beat faster. It read HAVE YOU SEEN THESE BOYS? and underneath was a grainy photo of Taylor and Jake fleeing from the Teton coach station.

Jake gasped. He had to get out of there fast. Pulling the flyer off the board, Jake shoved it into his pocket and started to cross the foyer of the information center. He prayed Garcia wouldn't notice him slipping out, but it was no use.

"Hey there! Wait a second!" Garcia had obviously put two and two together. "Aren't you—"

Jake didn't give the ranger a chance to finish his thought. He rushed outside and raced toward his brother and Cody.

"Did you get a map?" Taylor asked.

"Yeah, but we gotta get out of here *now*," Jake said.

"What about some food?"

"Just go!"

The boys made a break for it, darting into the nearest wooded area for cover. They circled back around the south end of Jenny Lake and followed the trail up the west shore about a mile and a half to Inspiration Point, until they were sweating from the effort. As they paused for breath, Jake explained to Taylor what he'd seen. It was clear that they had to be more careful now—people were looking for them.

As they approached Inspiration Point they could see that it was really just a little knob of land sticking out into the lake. Nearby was a boat dock for ferrying backpackers from the ranger station to the trailhead that led into the heart of the Tetons. The boys paused to again study the letter and the sketch their father had sent them—Jake was extra paranoid, looking around as if they'd be found out at any minute.

"Man, I am so hungry," Taylor moaned. "Don't we have any food left?"

Jake shook his head. "I wish."

"Couldn't we just go find a store and buy some supplies?"

"Don't you get it, Taylor?" Jake snapped, frustrated. "This is serious. We've already shown our faces more than we should have. If we show ourselves any more, someone's going to figure out who we are for sure. Now's not the time to be thinking of food!"

"I guess. . . . ," Taylor agreed.

"No, Taylor. For *certain*," Jake replied. "We have to be one step ahead of everyone—one false step, and we're finished. One false step, and we can forget about finding Dad . . . forever!"

14

With new determination, the boys followed the trail north, hugging the west side of Jenny Lake. They left Inspiration Point behind, just like their dad had said to in his letter. Passing smaller lakes along the way, they eventually headed toward the base of the mountains, keeping off the trail so as not to attract any attention. They scrambled through bushes and up and over rocks; fortunately, the terrain wasn't too steep. However, the lack of food quickly began to take a toll. Jake had to push himself up even small inclines, and Taylor fell farther and farther back. They had to find a base where they could rest for a while and think of how to get some food.

As they approached the three streams that fed into the lake, Jake heard Taylor suddenly yelp and cry, "Oh, gross!"

Jake spun around and hurried back to Taylor, fearing the worst.

Taylor held up his arm.

Jake expected to see a horrible gash or other wound, but instead his brother groaned, "Jake, a bird just pooped on me!"

Despite the gnawing in their stomachs, both brothers burst out laughing.

"I'm glad it picked you," said Jake. "Good thing it didn't hit your head."

Taylor gave him a glare. "It'll be aiming for you, next."

"Go ahead and wipe it off. We're almost there."

Taylor bent down to wipe the bird poop off on some lichen, but then paused to study it.

"What is it?" Jake asked.

"Jake, there're berry seeds in this poop!"

"So what? Let's—"

Then Jake realized what Taylor was getting at.

"Oh, I get it!" he told his brother. "Let's keep an eye out. If the bird found berries, there have to be more nearby."

As they made their way to the spot they'd picked out, they walked slowly, examining every shrub for berries. Soon, Taylor found a bush full of dark purple berries.

"They look like blueberries," he said. "Didn't Dad draw something like this in his journal?"

Jake quickly dug out the prized book and flipped to a drawing that showed the exact plant they were looking at.

Below the sketch, their dad had scrawled: *Huckleberry— safe!*

Taylor plucked one from the bush and popped it into his mouth.

"Wow! I've just found my new favorite food!"

He and Jake quickly stripped the bush and began avidly searching for others. Soon they came upon a different kind of plant, this one covered with thorns and red berries. Jake didn't need his father's journal to recognize this one.

"Raspberries!" he exclaimed.

"Oh yeah!" Taylor said, plucking off a couple of the riper fruits and popping them into his mouth. "Jake, I can get used to this."

The boys decided to collect as many of the berries as they could, using Jake's extra shirt as a bag. Jake moved ahead, carefully studying each of the bushes, while Cody and Taylor trailed behind him. They filled half of the T-shirt until they hit a stretch without any berry bushes at all. "Well, I don't see any more around," Jake said. "Taylor, what are you doing?"

As soon as Taylor turned around, Jake saw his brother put a glossy red berry into his mouth. His brother whipped his head toward Jake in surprise.

"What? I was just eating another berry."

"What kind was it?" Jake demanded, rushing up to him.

"I don't know. What's the difference? These others are all fine."

"Taylor, some berries are deadly poisonous. Spit it out!"

"What?"

"I'm serious—before that berry gets into your system."

Taylor spit the remains of the berries out onto the ground.

Jake handed Taylor the rest of his bottled water and studied the bush Taylor had eaten from. He again pulled out their father's journal and began flipping through pages. He stopped and showed the page to his brother.

Taylor swished a sip of water around in his mouth, then spit it out onto the ground. "'Baneberry—deadly!'" he read. Their father had underlined the word *deadly* three times.

"Jake—" Taylor was gasping, his face going pale even in the bright sunshine.

Jake threw his arm around his brother. "It's okay. We got lucky this time."

The boys continued walking through woods, up and over a rise, until they found themselves at the west end of Leigh Lake. Three separate creeks converged here, and as soon as the boys arrived, Jake saw a trout leap out of the lake and swallow a butterfly that had been flying too close to the surface of the water.

"This will be a good place to hang out for a while," Jake said. Despite Taylor's close call with the poisonous berries, the food in his system had revived his spirits. Taylor had recovered by now too.

"Where should we set up camp?" Taylor asked.

"Let's scout around."

Normally, Jake would have chosen a spot right next to the lake, but a hiking trail came down one of the drainages. It didn't look well used, but Jake didn't want to take any chances. Taylor, though, discovered a small clearing screened by trees.

"This will be perfect," Jake told him.

"I wish we had a tent," Taylor said.

But Jake had been thinking about that all day. He told Taylor about the beaver lodge he'd seen earlier.

"If a beaver can build a house made out of sticks, we should be able to," he said.

They began gathering thick branches and dead logs. Cody even got in on the act, dragging a branch after Taylor.

Then they found a small spruce that had been knocked sideways so that it lay parallel to the ground, at about head height with Jake.

"If we lean a bunch of these branches on top of this, it should give us a lean-to big enough to crawl under," Jake said.

Together they angled the larger branches against the fallen spruce, and then they began laying other branches perpendicular across that. It took them a while to figure out how to do it. More than once, several of the branches came loose and tumbled to the ground. Eventually, though, they'd created a fairly stable framework. With that in place, they began laying smaller branches filled with green needles over it all to form a thatch.

The boys and Cody crawled inside and looked at each other, grinning.

"Not bad," said Jake.

Cody also seemed to like it, and he eagerly sniffed every corner of their new home.

Taylor breathed in the sweet fresh scents of the green branches around them. "This is like the forts we used to build in the jungle back home—only better!"

Jake laughed. "Yeah. I forgot about those."

As they thought about home, the smiles faded from their faces. After a moment of silence, Taylor asked, "Jake, how do you think Mom's doing?"

Jake picked up a pine needle bundle and began peeling it apart. "I don't know. I'm sure the doctors at the hospital know what they're doing. I hope they can fix her up."

"But then what?" Taylor said. "She'll still be with Bull, won't she? What's to stop him from just beating her up again—or killing her?"

Jake didn't have an answer for that one.

"Jake, from here we can probably hike to a phone. Maybe we should do it—and get some more food while we're at it?"

Jake shook his head. "It's too risky. People are looking for us now: rangers, maybe even the cops. If we call anyone, they might trace the call. Then they'll find us for sure."

"We'll make the call short," said Taylor. "You know,

like they do in the movies. It takes them, like, thirty seconds to trace a call, doesn't it? If we use a pay phone and—"

"No!" Jake spoke more harshly than he'd intended. "Mom wouldn't want us to risk it either. If Bull finds out we're here with his money, it'll be bad. Real bad. And we're witnesses, Taylor—that makes us targets."

But Bull wasn't the only reason Jake didn't want to call home. He thought about how bloody and beaten their mom had looked on the gurney as they'd loaded her into the ambulance.

She might already be dead, he thought, swallowing hard. *If that's true, it'll be better if Taylor doesn't know—at least for now.*

He cleared his throat and said, "C'mon, let's get our stuff inside our new home."

The boys put their backpacks inside their shelter. Jake also hung the T-shirt containing the berries from a branch in the roof.

"That ought to keep it out of reach of squirrels and chipmunks," he said.

Taylor said, "Yeah. I already saw a couple of them around here. Do you think we could eat one?"

"Hmm." The thought had never occurred to Jake before, but it wasn't a bad idea. The darned things were so fast, though, he and Taylor would have to build some kind of a trap.

"That's a good idea," he told Taylor, "but it might be

easier to catch some fish first. Let's see if we can make a fishing pole and catch us and Cody a meal."

Both boys had learned to catch and clean fish the previous summer, but at camp they'd had modern rods and reels. Now they had nothing and were once again forced to improvise. They each found straight sticks about six feet long, and they cut off lengths of the string they'd brought for fishing line.

"What are we going to use for fishhooks?" Taylor asked.

"I don't know," said Jake. "Any ideas?"

Both boys began looking through their packs. Jake didn't find anything—not even wire. After a moment, however, Taylor pulled out a handful of paper clips.

"Hey, Jake. What about these?"

Jake laughed. "These just might work. Why don't you find some bait while I see what I can do with them?"

"You got it."

While Taylor went off into the trees with Cody, Jake began trying to turn one of the paper clips into a fishhook. His pocketknife had a little pair of pliers on it, which he used to fashion a loop to tie the paper clip to the string. Then he curled the other end of the paper clip so that it resembled a fishhook. He kept tinkering with the paper clip, bending down the very tip so that it formed a little barb.

That's about the best I can do, he thought, and then

proceeded to make three more of the little fishhooks.

Taylor returned. "Howsitgoin'?"

"Okay," Jake said, showing him the poles with the string and hooks attached.

"Cool! I caught a caterpillar and a couple of grass-hoppers for bait."

The boys took their poles down to the lakeside. The lake stretched more than a mile across, and as soon as they reached the shore, they saw another fish jump.

"That's what I'm talkin' about!" said Taylor.

Standing on some rocks that jutted out into the water, they baited their hooks with the grasshoppers, then cast their strings out into the water. Almost immediately, Jake felt a tug on his line.

"A fish!" he shouted.

Taylor also felt a tug. "Me too!"

Unfortunately, as soon as the boys tried to bring in their poles, the trout wriggled free.

"That's okay," said Jake. "Let's try it again."

The boys kept trying, but the paper clip hooks just wouldn't hold the fish. Finally Taylor threw his pole down in despair.

"This is never going to work, Jake. We need *real* fish-hooks."

Taylor stomped down the shore, with Cody trotting along behind him. Jake cast his line a couple more times, but then he gave up too.

"You're welcome for the free food," he told the trout as he headed back to camp. "I hope you enjoyed it."

Jake ate a few more berries, then tried to make the camp as comfortable as possible before the night ahead, while Taylor went foraging. All the while he was wracked with worry—if they didn't have something proper to eat soon, there'd be no chance of finding their father. They'd starve to death before they got anywhere near the moose's neck—if they could even figure out what the clues meant. Jake's stomach had long since gone past rumbling; instead it was starting to seize up.

"Jake, look what I found!" Taylor shouted as he returned to the camp.

Taylor held out four bird's eggs.

"Nice!" Jake exclaimed. "Where'd you find them?"

"I saw this bird. It looked like some kind of seabird. Cody and I started looking around, and we found these eggs."

"Good job, Taylor."

"The only thing is, we still don't have anything to make a fire with, do we?"

"Uh, no, but I suppose we could eat them raw."

The boys stared at each other, disgust twisting their mouths, but fresh pangs of hunger piercing their stomachs.

"You go first," Taylor said.

Still grimacing, Jake walked over to a nearby rock and squatted down next to it. Carefully, he cracked the shell and gently tore away half so that the raw egg sat cupped in the bottom half. The yellow and orange yolk quivered. Jake felt queasy just looking at it.

But this is what real mountain men do, he told himself, and brought the eggshell to his lips. With a quick movement, he threw his head back and tried to swallow the egg without tasting it.

It didn't work. The egg tasted like a big glob of snot as it slid down his throat. He coughed and sputtered.

"Blech!" he said.

Taylor's face scrunched up. "That bad?"

Jake shook it off. "Kinda. Your turn."

Taylor followed Jake's example and quickly washed out his mouth with water from his water bottle.

"Yech."

"Yeah, I know. I'm thinking we should give the other two eggs to Cody."

Taylor looked at him. "I was thinking the same thing."

By now the sky was beginning to darken, and it was time to think about making some sort of bed for their shelter. The boys gathered fresh pine boughs and leaves, and made themselves as comfortable and warm as possible.

Cody crawled into their shelter with them. Their new bed actually felt quite warm, especially when they were curled up with Cody.

"This isn't bad," Taylor said.

"Yeah." Jake was proud of what they'd accomplished so far. They had shelter and warmth. Hunger was their main problem, but he planned to launch a fresh attack on the trout the next day. Once they figured that out, they could resume the search for their dad's clues. Feeling optimistic, Jake drifted off to sleep.

But six hours later he was woken with a crash.

15

"What's happening, Jake?" Taylor shouted.

A thick crossbeam from their shelter fell onto Jake's shoulders, and Cody started barking and snarling. Jake tried to sit up but smacked his head against another tree branch.

"Taylor, are you all right?" he said, struggling in the blackness to work out where he was.

"I don't know! Where are you?"

Cody continued to bark and snarl, now moving a few feet away. But Jake heard other sounds too. Deep snuffling and murmuring. It sounded like an animal of some sort . . . something big. *Really* big.

"Jake, there's something next to us!"

Right as Taylor spoke, the entire shelter crashed down on top of them, and a terrifying growl filled their ears.

"Grab on to me!" Jake shouted, but as he did so, something big, heavy, and furry brushed his shoulder. More of their shelter fell, and Jake reached wildly for his brother, clambering up off the ground.

"Taylor, where are you?" Jake shouted as a smaller branch whacked his head.

"I'm here!" Taylor cried, and suddenly Jake felt his brother's fingers lock into his.

"Quick! Get out of here!"

The boys scrambled and clawed their way out of the pile of logs and sticks, and stood up. Cody continued to bark furiously, and finally the boys could see why.

Lit only by dim starlight, the animal looked huge. It puffed and panted like a locomotive—an *angry* locomotive—and it flung branches and sticks aside as if they were straw. *A bear!* And with a roar, it surged forward.

"It's coming after us!" Taylor shouted. "Run!"

Without thinking, the boys scrambled back and scurried farther into the trees.

"Stand back to back and make lots of noise!" Jake shouted.

The boys started yelling at the top of their lungs, Cody barking right next to them, ready to take on the bear. They even waved their clothes in the air, trying to make themselves look as big as possible. Both brothers braced for the bear attack, but the noise of their hollering made the bear retreat, and after a few seconds it drifted back toward their camp.

Taylor peered around a tree trunk toward what remained of their shelter. "Jake, what's it *doing*?"

Jake watched as the bear took apart the shelter. "The berries!" he realized. "It's not after us. It's after the berries we picked!"

Almost as if it knew the boys were talking about it, the bear stopped clawing through their shelter and peered back in their direction.

"Uh-oh!" Taylor said.

But at that instant, Cody raced out to circle behind the bear and nip its back leg. The bear wheeled and swiped at the pesky terrier. As Cody sprang back, the bear followed it away from where the brothers hid.

"Careful, Cody!" Taylor called, but the little dog knew what it was doing. Barking, it led the bear away from their camp. Whenever the bear paused or turned back toward the shelter, Cody leaped in and nipped at it again. Gradually, the sounds of Cody and the bear faded into the distance.

Cautiously, Jake and Taylor returned to their shelter. The bear had transformed it into a pile of kindling and splinters.

"Geez!" Taylor said, his breathing still rapid. "That was close."

"Yeah," Jake agreed. "That'll teach us to leave food where we sleep. At least it wasn't a grizzly bear."

"How can you tell? That thing looked huge."

"Grizzlies have big humps on their backs and are twice as big as that. That was definitely a black bear—fortunately."

"Good thing Cody was here."

"Yeah—again!"

Taylor picked up one of the logs from the shelter. "I wish I were as brave as him!"

On cue, Cody trotted back into camp, wagging his tail as if nothing had happened. Taylor petted him and gave him what was left of the berry stash as a fiery orange line began tracing the hills to the east.

"It's getting light," Taylor said.

Jake swatted at a mosquito. "Yeah, we should keep going."

"Okay, but I gotta have some food soon," Taylor whined.

Jake nodded. *If we're going to keep looking for Dad, we've got to get some protein. Get our strength back.*

"Well," he said, "what do you say we rebuild the shelter, then go after those trout again?"

"Do you think the bear will come back?" Taylor asked.

"Not with Cody here," Jake said. Although he sounded much more confident than he felt.

The boys spent the next few hours rebuilding their shelter. It went more quickly now that they'd figured out what worked and what didn't. By the time the sun separated from the horizon, they'd erased all traces of the bear.

Now, to catch some fish, Jake told himself.

Taylor decided to try to make a spear to stab some of the trout, and while he went to search for a long straight pole, Jake sat down with his father's journal and flipped through it for other ideas. His dad had used two pages to sketch out the best lures to use and how best to tie on fishhooks.

"That would be great if we had any fishhooks," Jake muttered.

On the next page, though, his father had sketched a tool that just might be useful—a net or scoop made with a forked branch and a T-shirt spread between the branches. Jake had always skimmed over that page before, but now it caught his attention.

"Ah . . ." For the first time, it occurred to him that he might be able to net some fish instead of trying to catch them with hook and line, and he quickly set about creating the tool his father had drawn. Meanwhile, Taylor returned with a long straight pole and began using his pocketknife to whittle the end into a sharp point.

Soon the boys were ready to resume battle.

"Well, the fish are definitely there," said Jake, seeing one leap out of the water as they walked toward the lake-shore.

"They look hungry, too," said Taylor. "Let's spread out. I'll go this way, and you go that way. Whoever catches the most fish gets to pick what they want to watch on televi-sion tonight."

Jake laughed. "Very funny," he said, and began walking counterclockwise along the shore, looking for a likely spot to ambush some trout. He found another rock that stuck out into the lake and decided to lie down and wait for the fish to come to him. The water next to the rock was about two feet deep, and he watched minnows and dace lazily swim by or dart quickly when they got excited. Soon a ten-inch trout approached, attracted by the shade of the rock.

Jake tightened his grip on the net, ready to plunge it under the water after the fish. The fish drifted closer and closer.

Splash!

Jake thrust the scoop under the water and quickly pulled it back up, splashing water all over his face. When he opened his eyes, he saw . . .

Nothing.

No fish. Just the wet T-shirt hanging limply between the forked branches of the net.

Jake glanced over at Taylor in time to see him throw his spear into the water, but his brother also came up empty-handed.

"We've got to be quicker," Jake muttered.

He lay back down on the rock again and waited. Twice more, trout drifted close. Twice more, Jake failed to net one.

"Shoot!" Jake said, standing up. There were fewer mosquitoes now that the sun's heat was building around the lake. Unfortunately, that meant the fish had moved off to deeper, cooler waters away from the shore. Jake's stomach rumbled fiercely.

We've got to catch something, or we'll have to risk heading back into town for groceries—or starve!

He watched another trout leap out of the water after an insect, and suddenly he got an idea. He quickly set to work, picking up large rocks and setting them underwater, until just their tops reached the surface.

"What are you doing?" Taylor said, returning with Cody.

"I'm building a fish trap," Jake told him. "Grab some rocks."

Taylor quickly grasped the plan. Together they built two fences of rocks, reaching out from the shoreline. At the point where the two arcs would meet, they left an opening about eighteen inches wide.

"Now we've got to bait it," said Jake. "You're the bait expert."

Taylor took Cody to catch some more grasshoppers while Jake found a rock he could quickly drop into the trap opening to block it. When Taylor returned, they tossed a couple of the grasshoppers as far out into the water as they could. Within moments, they saw a splash as a fish seized one of them.

"Now throw a few inside the trap," Jake said.

Taylor tossed two more grasshoppers right inside the trap opening. After a minute the boys spotted a fish swim into the trap and swallow the grasshopper.

Jake reached out and squeezed Taylor's arm. "It's working! Throw another one," he whispered.

Taylor continued tossing grasshoppers, and two more fish swam into the trap. Picking up the rock door, Jake slowly circled around to the trap entrance. The trout saw him and swam excitedly to get away, but they didn't know where the opening was and kept running up against the trap's rock walls.

Jake dropped the rock "door" in place. "Taylor, get the net!"

Taylor picked it up and waded into the trap. The fish swam frantically now, zipping back and forth past his legs. Jake jumped in too, and together the brothers managed to corner one of the fish. Cody barked with excitement.

"Now!" Jake shouted.

Taylor plunged the net underwater. Twisting and splashing as the trout tried to make an escape, Taylor held on firmly and gathered up the fish in the T-shirt. Heaving upward, he opened the shirt to reveal a twelve-inch brook trout, its colorful spots gleaming in the sun.

"I got it, Jake! I got it!"

16

"What a catch!" Jake whooped.

Together they grasped the wriggling fish and hurried to shore, where they quickly killed it with a rock. Running back and wading into the water, the brothers caught the other two fish trapped against the rock walls.

Taylor whooped, his calls echoing across the lake.

Jake was too happy to warn him to keep his voice down, and together they used their pocketknives to gut and clean the fish, then took them back to camp.

"Man, am I hungry," Taylor said. "How are we going to cook them?"

Jake had been so elated about catching the fish that he'd momentarily forgotten that they had to cook them too.

"Well, we could eat them raw."

The brothers exchanged glances, and they both scrunched up their mouths at the memory of the raw bird's eggs.

"Well," said Taylor, "maybe not."

Jake looked down at the trout and saw an ant crawling over one of them. He reached out to flick it away.

"Hey," said Taylor. "I got an idea."

Jake looked at his brother. "You know how we can start a fire?"

"Yeah, Jake. Remember that weird kid Joey in our neighborhood?"

"Sure."

"Well, one time I saw him burning ants with a magnifying glass. What if we do the same thing, just without the ants?"

Jake's face brightened. "That's right! I remember you telling me about that. That's brilliant, Taylor!"

The boys quickly gathered a variety of kindling—everything from small twigs and dried leaves to thicker sticks that they could layer up. They cleared a circle of ground, then Taylor brought out his pocketknife and unfolded one of the tools on the knife: a tiny magnifying glass.

"What should we try to burn first?" Taylor asked.

"This oughta work," Jake said, pulling out a used napkin he'd stuffed into his pocket back at the truck stop. "Yeah!"

With the sun almost directly overhead, Taylor was able

to focus a tiny, intense beam down on the napkin. Within seconds, the paper began to smoke and turn brown. Then it burst into a tiny flame.

"That's it!" said Jake, laying some twigs across the burning paper. He remembered from camp that the trick to getting a fire going was to give it fuel, but to allow enough space for oxygen to reach the flames. At first he thought he'd smothered the faint flame; then one of the tiny twigs caught fire.

"It's still going!" Taylor enthused. "Give it some more wood."

The boys kept putting bigger and bigger sticks on the fire until they had a steady blaze.

"Man, that's the prettiest thing I've ever seen," said Taylor.

Jake had to agree.

Since they didn't have any cooking utensils, they skewered the fish on sticks and held them over the fire.

"This is like roasting marshmallows," Taylor said. "Only better."

"Yeah," Jake said, giving Cody a scratch with his free hand. Already, his mouth watered at the prospect of eating his first real meal in two days. The boys had cooked bluegill at camp the previous summer, but they'd had a frying pan and butter for those. They weren't sure how long a trout was supposed to cook, so they held the fish over the flames until the skins had turned crisp and black. Then they began picking the flesh off with their fingers.

"Oh, that's *good*," Taylor moaned, slurping down a bite.

"Yeah," said Jake. "Right now I'm pretty sure it's the best food on earth!"

Taylor laughed and fed a couple bites of fish to Cody, who sat begging for more.

"Best of all," he said, "that lake is full of fish. When we're done, let's go back and get some more."

"No arguments here," said Jake. *If we'd gone much longer without decent food, we'd be finished,* he thought.

Just then, though, a loud voice called, "Hey, you! What are you doing over there?"

"Crap!" Jake said, leaping to his feet, followed immediately by Taylor and Cody.

A man in a dark green pants and a gray button-down shirt stepped out of the trees only thirty feet away.

"What are you boys doing here?" the ranger repeated, approaching them.

Cody growled softly.

"Uh, nothing," Taylor said.

"We were just building a campfire to keep the mosquitoes away," said Jake.

"Do you have a backcountry camping permit?"

"Uh—" Taylor began, but Jake cut him off.

"We didn't realize we needed it," said Jake. "Can you give us one?"

The ranger studied them. "How old are you boys, and where are your parents?"

"They're, um, camping back down the road. We're supposed to join up with them later."

The ranger frowned. He said, "Well, you're breaking about five park regulations right now, including camping without a permit, building an open fire in an undesignated location, having a dog in bear country, and from what I can see, fishing without a license. I don't suppose you have one of those either, do you?"

"We lost it," Taylor blurted out.

Great, Jake thought. *Why not just tell him that Cody ate it?*

The ranger made a small murmuring sound and then said, "I see. Well, in that case, I think we need to put this fire out. Then you boys will have to come with me."

Jake's heart thundered.

If we go with him, he'll figure out who we are and send us back to Bull. We'll never find Dad.

"We didn't mean to do anything wrong," Jake said.

"I'm sure you didn't," said the ranger. "But rules are rules."

"Can we just get our stuff? It's right over there." Jake pointed toward their shelter.

The ranger nodded. "But make it snappy. We've got to put out this fire."

"O-okay. Thanks."

Jake, Taylor, and Cody walked toward their shelter. Jake could feel the ranger's eyes following them, and then heard the ranger speaking on his radio.

"Jake, what are we going to do?" Taylor whispered.

"How fast can you run?" Jake whispered back.

They reached their shelter and quickly stuffed their packs with their belongings.

"What about the berries?" Taylor whispered.

"Leave 'em. We can find more."

"You kids ready yet?" the ranger called.

Jake glanced over to see the man walking toward them.

"Now!" Jake shouted. "Fast!"

17

The boys set off running, Cody close behind. They scrambled through some trees and made their way back down to the lakeshore. The ranger hollered at them again, and Jake thought he heard footsteps, but when he looked back, he saw that the man had given up the chase. Instead he was talking into his radio.

"We've got to find someplace to hide—and fast!" Jake told his brother.

"Yeah, but where?"

Jake quickly studied the lakeshore in front of them. It ran east–west, but a steep mountain slope came down to meet it from the north, leaving only a thin strip to walk along.

An easy place to get trapped by another ranger.

Their only other choice was to follow one of the creek

drainages that dropped down to the lake. Jake didn't know where it led, but he made a quick decision.

"C'mon," he told Taylor. "Up here."

"Where's this go?"

"I don't know, but if we stay next to the lake, they'll catch us for sure."

They hurried up the rocky ravine. Though a few trees clung to the ridges above, the stream bed and its banks were rocky and exposed.

"Do you think they'll send a helicopter to find us?" Taylor asked, reading Jake's mind.

"I don't know," said Jake, already gasping from the climb.

Must be the altitude, he thought. The Tetons weren't Mount Everest, but they had to be a lot higher above sea level than Pittsburgh.

Taylor's chest also heaved with the effort. Only Cody seemed to take the climb in stride.

They kept following the little stream as it grew even steeper. Soon they found themselves at the base of a large scree field. To their left, the route kept climbing up to a moonscape of rock and snow. Without a tree in sight, there was nowhere to hide.

Not a place we want to get stuck, Jake thought.

To the right, however, the brothers could see a small ridge that might just lead to somewhere better.

"What about up there?" Taylor pointed, panting.

Jake took another thin gulp of air. "Uh . . . yeah."

The trio left the stream and began scrambling up the steep slope on their right. It was tough going. The scree slid out from under their shoes, and they were soon using both their hands and feet to make their way.

"I feel like a mountain goat," Taylor said, gasping.

Jake was sucking in too much air to answer. After fifteen minutes, though, they reached the upper section of the ridge. The boys paused, exhausted, and collapsed onto the rocky ground.

"Wow," Jake said.

From where they sat, they looked down on a small valley. Even though it was July, a snowfield filled more than half of it. Below that, a small stream of meltwater flowed down the valley, eventually entering a lake much larger than any they'd seen so far.

"Is that Jackson Lake?" Taylor asked, pulling his water bottle from his pack. He took a big swig and then handed it to his brother. Jake also gulped noisily from the bottle, and then he took out the topographic map he'd gotten at the ranger station.

Taylor crowded in to look over his shoulder while Jake traced their route.

"Yep. That's Jackson Lake, all right," said Jake.

"Man, it's huge!"

"According to this map, it's about five miles across and ten miles long.""Do you think this is where the waterfall is?" Taylor asked. "The one Dad told us to find?"

"Maybe," said Jake. "But I don't know how we're going to find it. I don't know what Dad was thinking. 'Look across the moose's neck'? I mean, c'mon."

"Well, there's gotta be moose down there," Taylor said.

"Sure, but I don't think Dad was talking about a real moose, do you?"

Taylor shrugged. "Only way to know what he meant is to start searching."

Jake sighed. He knew Taylor was right, but looking at the size of the area they had to cover made him feel more doubtful than ever that they could find their father.

"Let's go down to the lake and set up a new camp," said Taylor. "I want to catch some more fish. I could have eaten ten of those!"

"It's too risky," said Jake. "Even if they don't send a helicopter, the rangers will be looking for us by now. We'd better find someplace to hide tonight."

Taylor nodded reluctantly. The boys and Cody began descending the other side of the ridge. They walked down to the snowfield and, just for fun, crunched their way across it. Then they followed the snowmelt stream down through a small shallow valley toward Jackson Lake. Instead of continuing down to the lake, however, they turned north and walked toward another rocky ridge. On their left, they saw an even larger snow and ice field.

"Is that a glacier?" Taylor wondered.

Jake again consulted the map. "Yeah, I think it is."

"Wish I had a camera," said Taylor. "Mom would never believe that her boys were standing beneath a real live glacier."

At the mention of their mother, both boys fell silent.

Is she even alive? Jake thought, but he kept his question to himself.

They continued walking, climbing the next steep rocky ridge. Again, it was a tough slog, and again, the boys stopped at the top, gasping for air. Below them, though, they saw a hidden depression—a cirque carved by long-gone glaciers, according to their father's journal.

"You think we should hide down there tonight?"

Jake glanced up at the sky, and for the first time noticed heavy clouds rolling in.

"Yeah," Jake said. "It'll be dark in a couple of hours."

Making their way into the cirque proved easier said than done. The boys had to carefully pick their way down the steep slope, and both brothers slid on the loose rock several times. Only Cody remained sure-footed, and he kept turning around as if to say, *What's keeping you slackers?*

They made it into the cirque just as real darkness began closing in and, almost immediately, the temperature began falling. The trio explored the area for some sort of shelter, but they didn't find much. Eventually they found a rock overhang—not even a cave—that just might offer some protection. Unfortunately, the gathering clouds immediately put that to the test.

Jake felt a fat drop of water hit him on the bridge of the nose. Several more followed. Then frozen pellets began raining down on them.

"Hail!" Jake said. "Quick, into the cave."

The boys ducked under the overhang and put on every piece of clothing they owned. As they were pulling on their raincoats, several pieces of hail tumbled down their necks and under their T-shirts.

"Brrr!" Taylor said, but both he and Jake started laughing. "One minute it's hot, the next, there's hailstones! Can you believe it?"

Even though he'd never experienced it before, Jake had read how unpredictable mountain weather could be. He, Taylor, and Cody burrowed even deeper into their shelter.

Suddenly the brothers saw a flash, like a giant camera going off. Two seconds later, a deafening blast shook the glacial cirque. Taylor and Jake looked at each other, astonished, while Cody burrowed deep between them.

Almost immediately, they saw a bolt of lightning strike the ridge on the opposite side of the cirque, and another cannon blast of thunder assaulted them.

"Man, this is better than the fireworks back home!" Taylor shouted over the roar of the storm.

Jake nodded, but he wasn't enjoying the display quite as much as his brother. *What would Mom think, knowing that we were here now? If we'd stayed in Pittsburgh, at least we'd have food and a warm bed.*

Then he thought of Bull.

No, he corrected himself. *That psychopath would have found a way to get to us. As rough as this is, we're better off here—no matter how dangerous it is.*

The boys continued to watch the spectacular lightning show. At one point, they saw a brilliant blue-white bolt strike a tree on the opposite ridge. He couldn't tell for sure, but Jake thought he saw the tree glow orange and shatter the instant the lightning hit it.

When the storm finally moved on, it left the tiny valley eerily quiet. Then Jake heard something that made him snap to attention.

"Jake, did you hear that?"

"Yeah—what was it?" Jake murmured. The boys listened hard and then heard the cry once more, clearly this time.

"Jake!" Taylor said, straightening up. "Someone's calling for help!"

18

With Cody in the lead, the brothers scrambled out from under their overhang. By now the clouds had cleared, and the light from the waxing quarter moon illuminated the area with a surprisingly brilliant glow.

"Which way was it coming from?" Jake asked.

"Across there, I think. Near those trees."

The boys made their way to the other side of the cirque and paused, listening.

"Help!" a strained voice called out.

Following Cody, the boys reached the edge of a small group of trees at the base of a rocky slope. There, they found a man lying on the rough ground, his right arm pinned under a boulder the size of their dishwasher back home.

Cody barked and ran up to the man, then licked his grizzled face.

"Geez!" Taylor exclaimed. "What happened?"

The man grunted in pain. "Wouldn't believe me if I told you. Can you get this rock off me?"

"Yeah, sure! Help me, Jake!"

Together the boys squatted on either side of the man and reached under the edges of the boulder.

"On three," Jake said. "One, two, three, *lift*!"

The boys grunted together, pushing off with their legs.

The boulder didn't budge.

"Don't think you're gonna get her like that," the man said. "Get the rope outta my pack."

A few yards away lay a large well-worn internal frame backpack.

"Right pocket," the man instructed.

Jake unzipped the side pocket of the pack and pulled out a length of nylon climbing rope.

"Either of you know how to tie a bowline knot?" the man asked.

"We both do," said Taylor. "We learned it at camp last summer."

"Good," said the man, gasping. "Tie a big loop around the edge of this boulder with a bowline knot. Then toss the other end of the rope over that tree branch there."

The boys immediately saw what the man was getting at, and five minutes later they had assembled a makeshift pulley.

"Okay, let's try it again," Jake told Taylor. "One, two, *three!*" They pulled on the rope.

"It's budging," the man called. "Just a little more."

"Harder, Jake!" Taylor shouted.

The boys redoubled their efforts. The branch of the tree creaked under the strain of the rope, but a second later the rock shifted and the man cried out in pain and relief, "I'm free!"

Jake and Taylor released the rope, and the boulder settled back with a dull thud. The boys hurried to the man, who now sat dazed, grasping his right forearm.

"Are you all right?" Taylor asked.

The man growled like a bear. "I'm alive, thanks to you boys, but I think I've got a broken arm."

Even in the moonlight, Jake could see that the arm looked swollen and, despite the cold air, the man sweated with pain. "What can we do to help?"

The man grunted again. "I think you're going have to splint it for me. You know how to do that?"

Jake shook his head. "No. We didn't get that far in first aid."

"Okay, then. You're going to need a straight, wide stick, about a foot long, and a few strips of cloth. You can tear up one of my shirts in the pack there."

While the boys worked, they asked the man what had happened.

"I was tracking Felix with the antenna there," the man

said, nodding to a smashed-up framework of wires and poles on the nearby ground.

"Who's Felix?" Taylor asked, holding the piece of wood firmly under the man's forearm.

"Felix is a wolverine," the man told them. "One of about a dozen living in the Tetons–Yellowstone area. Anyway, he was on the move, and I was scrambling up those rocks, trying to keep up, when that storm moved in. Felix came straight down this steep slope, and I scurried down after him."

"You mean during the hailstorm?" Jake asked, tying the second of four pieces of cotton cloth to hold the splint in place. The man winced as Jake pulled the knot snug.

"Yeah," he continued. "I was scrambling down when a bolt of lightning hit right there above us. Set off a rockslide that knocked my feet out from under me. Next thing I knew, I was lying on my back, pinned under this boulder like the tail pinned on—or under—a donkey!"

"You're lucky those rocks didn't bury you!" Taylor told him.

"You got that right—thank God you showed up!"

Jake tied off the last of the splint and then, following the man's instructions, helped tie a sling with the rest of the spare shirt. The man tested it and murmured with approval.

"Not a bad field dressing. Maybe I should bring you guys along on all my tracking trips. Name's Skeet, by the way."

The man held out his good hand.

Jake shook it. "Uh, nice to meet you." Despite having

just saved the man's life, Jake felt reluctant to reveal his and Taylor's identities. For once, Taylor picked up on Jake's cue. To turn the attention away from themselves, Jake said, "You said you were tracking here. You were hunting the wolverine? To eat?"

The man chortled. "I don't think they'd taste very good. You ever seen a wolverine?"

The boys shook their heads.

"They're not much bigger than your buddy there," he said, pointing to Cody. "But pound-for-pound, they're the strongest, fiercest animals in the mountains here. I'd take on a grizzly bear any day before I'd face down an angry wolverine."

Looking at the man, Jake could imagine him tackling either one. In addition to his deely tanned face, he had long hair pulled back into a ponytail and a long salt-and-pepper beard. The man's muscles stood out from his arms and neck like steel bridge cables.

"Anyway," Skeet continued, "the park service pays me to follow and collect data on wolverines in the area. The wolverines are about the most rare and endangered mammal in the lower forty-eight."

"Endangered? How come?" Taylor asked.

"They used to be trapped and hunted. Now global warming is melting off a lot of the snowfields they need to survive. Anyway," the man said, struggling to his feet, "enough about me. What are you two boys doing out here all alone?"

Again, Jake and Taylor glanced at each other, neither one responding. Skeet picked up on it.

"Okay, I get it," he said. "But let me ask you this: would either of you object to a hot bath and a warm meal?"

The brothers broke into a grin, and Jake's stomach rumbled so loudly, he thought he could hear it echo off the walls of the cirque.

"That's what I figured," said Skeet. "If one of you can carry my pack, I'll lead the way."

While Taylor went back to the overhang to retrieve their own packs, Jake found Skeet a good walking stick and gave him a painkiller from his first aid kit. Then Jake hoisted the man's pack. It was heavy—maybe fifty pounds—but a lot more comfortable than the flimsy things he and Taylor had been hauling around. When Taylor returned, the group set off following a small stream toward Jackson Lake.

In the bright moonlight, Skeet had no trouble leading them. Every once in a while, he took a bad step and grunted or winced in pain, but they made swift progress to the lake, where they picked up a well-worn hiking trail. Soon after, they arrived at a beat-up green International pickup truck parked at the end of a little-used gravel track.

"This isn't an official parking area, but the park service guys all recognize the Green Monster here and leave 'er alone," Skeet told them. "Just throw the packs in the back. Either of you fellas drive a stick shift?"

"We don't drive at all," Taylor blurted.

Skeet frowned, then looked up at the setting moon and sky full of stars. "Well, the good news is it's a great night to start learning. My gear-shifting arm's no good, but if one of you can shift, I think I can manage the pedals and steering wheel. Who wants to give shifting a whirl?"

Jake was about to volunteer, but he looked at Taylor and said, "You do it."

Taylor's face lit up. "Really, Jake?" he asked, forgetting to conceal their names.

Jake nodded. "Yeah, Taylor. Go ahead." He figured there was no longer any reason not to use Taylor's name.

With Skeet's instructions, Taylor quickly figured out the truck's ancient manual transmission. At first the gears gave off hideous grinding noises whenever he shifted, and once, while he was instructing Taylor, Skeet almost steered straight into a ponderosa pine. By the time they drove out of the park, however, Taylor was only grinding the gears every third or fourth shift.

"Maybe we should try out for the NASCAR circuit," Skeet joked.

They drove about ten miles beyond the park's border before turning onto a series of logging roads. They navigated the Green Monster along smaller and smaller roads before finally pulling the truck up to a small cabin made of hand-cut timbers.

"Home, sweet home!" Skeet climbed out of the truck,

again wincing in pain, while Jake and Taylor pulled the backpacks from the truck.

"Good job driving," Jake told Taylor as Skeet led them to the cabin. Taylor beamed.

Skeet pushed through the cabin door and opened a couple of shutters to let in some light. "It isn't much," he said, "but it's all mine and it's hard to find."

Jake put down their packs, and he and Taylor stared in wonder at the cabin. They saw hardly any lights or electrical appliances anywhere, but dominating the center of the far wall was an old woodburning stove with a black cylindrical pipe rising through the ceiling. To one side stood a simple bed, built from wrist-thick logs, and on the other side, next to a window, sat a handmade wooden table with three wooden chairs surrounding it.

The cabin's walls, though, really caught the boys' attention. Dozens of wooden pegs had been inserted into the log beams, and from them hung an astounding assortment of tools, traps, weapons, lamps, rope, pots, frying pans—everything a person needed to survive. On the walls next to the door, Skeet had built several shelves loaded with jars of canned fruits and vegetables and meats, along with flour, sugar, molasses, rice, and other staples.

"Cool!" Taylor exclaimed.

Cody obviously agreed, and set about sniffing two large bearskin rugs spread across the cabin floor.

Jake said, "You must have been living out here for a long time."

"Yep," Skeet said. "But we've got plenty of time to chat later. You boys fix us some breakfast while I find a proper splint for this arm here."

Skeet dug out an enormous first aid box that seemed hopelessly modern compared to the rest of the cabin. Armed with real matches for a change, Taylor quickly got a fire going in the wood stove, while Jake took out a frying pan and began studying the shelves.

"Why don't you open a couple of cans of corned beef and hash?" Skeet suggested. "Then head out to the cold box. I think I got a few eggs in there."

Outside, Jake found a wooden storage box sunk deeply into the north side of the hill. He unlatched the two wooden bolts on the door, and inside, he found a dozen eggs along with two sides of what looked like cured deer meat. By the time he got back, Taylor had the fire blazing, so Jake dumped half the eggs and the corned beef into the frying pan and soon had the mixture sizzling away on the stove. Fifteen minutes later, they all sat down to breakfast.

"Not bad," Skeet said, shoving a big spoonful of eggs and hash into his mouth. "It seems like you've done this before."

"Our mom's been sick," Taylor explained between bites. "Jake here does most of the cooking."

Skeet nodded, and they all finished eating in silence.

Afterward, Skeet told them to fill up two large pots of water from the well outside. "It's to wash the dishes," he explained. "And I imagine you boys could use a bath, too, eh? I've got a few solar panels on the roof, and later in the day they'll turn out some warm water, but for now, we'll just have to make do with the stove."

After the heavy meal, fatigue had begun to settle in, but they did as Skeet told them, boiling the water, cleaning up the dishes, and then mixing the rest of the hot water with cold water in a large steel tub about fifty feet from the cabin.

By the time they'd washed and hung up their clothes, Jake and Taylor were so tired, they could barely stand up straight. Skeet didn't look much peppier. Even though the sun had climbed well above the tree line, Skeet said, "Well, boys, now that the chores are done, I think we could all use a little shut-eye, don't you agree?"

"You got that right," Taylor said, sighing.

Jake and Skeet smiled.

"All right. You boys make yourselves at home. I've got a couple of extra sleeping bags you can spread out on the bearskins there. Sleep as long as you want, and when we all feel like ourselves again, we'll sit down and have a talk."

19

When Jake opened his eyes, he didn't know where he was or how long he'd been sleeping. A dim light filtered in through the cabin windows, and he breathed in the musky scents of the bearskins beneath him. To his side, Taylor snored deeply, but Skeet's bed was empty. Jake thought maybe he'd slept almost an entire day and that it was dawn once again, but a few moments later he heard footsteps approach the cabin from outside, and the heavy wooden door squeaked open.

"Anyone alive in here?" Skeet asked.

Jake sat up. "Uh, yeah. Is it morning?"

Skeet chuckled. "No, but we burned most of the daylight. Kick that brother of yours, and come help me check the traplines."

Skeet left again while Jake managed to rouse Taylor. Outside, they found Skeet sitting at a rough-made table under a ponderosa pine—a collection of maps and note-books were spread out before him. Nearby, Jake noticed a solar panel recharging some batteries—presumably for some of Skeet's equipment.

"What are you doing?" Jake asked.

"Just catching up on my notes from my latest tracking trip in the Tetons."

"You mean looking for the wolverines?" Taylor asked, still rubbing grit from his eyes.

"Yep. Unfortunately, that rockslide smashed all my tracking gear. I'm going to need a new antenna and receiver."

"Is that how you follow them? With a radio?" Jake had heard about scientists who radio-collared wild animals, but he had never actually met one.

"Yep. Got about a dozen wolverines collared, but for the last week or so, I've been following Felix. He's a young male and seems to be lookin' for a new territory. I hope I don't lose him while I'm getting this gear replaced."

"Doesn't your arm need to get better too?"

Skeet glanced down at his sling and scoffed. "Baw, this isn't anything—probably just a hairline fracture. It won't slow me down too much," Skeet said, standing up. "In fact, while you two were sawin' logs, I managed to set a few traps, even with my lame arm here. Let's go see if we caught ourselves some dinner."

"I thought you wanted to talk," said Taylor.

"First rule of survival: chores come first."

Skeet led them over rough ground for about a mile. Instead of following trails, they crossed exposed granite slopes and cut through stands of pine and fir that looked like no human had set foot there before. The sun had dipped behind mountain peaks to the west, but this time of year, the sky held on to plenty of light to help them find their way. As they walked, they flushed a mule deer and a small flock of turkeys.

"Watch where you step," Skeet cautioned them. "The way you fellas walk, every animal within ten miles of here knows you're coming—don't you want some grub?"

After that, Jake and Taylor did their best to start stepping on rocks and avoid twigs that would make noise, but only Cody seemed to move as quietly as Skeet. Finally Skeet held up his hand, and the boys slowed. They cautiously approached a game trail where Skeet had set his first trap.

"Gather round," he told them. "I want to show you this."

The boys squatted down next to a large flat rock held up by a trio of sticks and arranged like the number four, with one of the sticks anchored into the ground.

"How is that thing even holding up the rock?" Taylor asked, studying the design.

"Pure physics," Skeet said. "By cutting the notches in the right way, you create a trigger. When a rabbit or some other critter comes to check out the bait on the part of the stick under the rock, it knocks all the sticks loose, letting the rock fall."

"But you didn't catch anything in this one," Taylor said.

Skeet grunted. "No. Was hoping for a rabbit, but I was in a hurry. Maybe the rabbit smelled me."

"Smelled you?" Jake asked.

"Yeah. When you set a trap, you have to do your best to cover your scent. I usually rub my hands and the parts of the trap in dirt or against a piece of charred wood from a fire. You can also find yourself a sage plant and rub the leaves over your skin, but with my bad arm here, I skipped that today. Anyway, go ahead and trigger this thing."

Taylor picked up a short dead tree branch and carefully pressed down on the baited end of the stick under the trap. In an instant, the rock slammed down on the ground. Jake and Taylor flinched and looked at each other, their mouths open.

"Wow!" said Taylor. "That trap really works!"

"Why'd you want to trigger it?" asked Jake.

"Well, we wouldn't be back to check it again until morning. By that time something else would probably eat anything we killed. Also, these traps don't always kill an animal right away. We wouldn't want an animal to suffer all night if it's only injured."

They left the trap and began walking through more trees.

"There are other kinds of traps, aren't there?" Jake asked as they walked. "I've read about snare traps before."

"Oh yeah," Skeet answered. "There're all kinds of snares, from spring-loaded snares to drag snares to simple snares that just hold an animal. I don't like to use 'em, though."

"Why not?" Taylor asked. "Don't they work?"

"Oh, they work great, but they don't usually kill the animal outright. Animals can get caught and struggle for hours—sometimes days. These deadfall traps I set up usually kill an animal instantly. It doesn't suffer. Speaking of which . . ."

Skeet again slowed as they approached another boulder.

"Looks like we might get lucky here," Skeet said. "You fellas, lift up that rock. I had a heck of a time just setting up this one with my hurt arm."

Together the boys lifted up the rock to find a dead animal under it.

"Whoa!" Taylor exclaimed. "A rabbit!"

"Snowshoe hare, actually," Skeet said. "Boys, meet your dinner."

"I thought snowshoe hares were white," Jake said as Cody stepped forward to sniff the dead mammal.

"Only in winter. That brown fur is its summer coloration. One of you boys, carry it while we check our last trap."

The last trap was empty, so Jake sprang it, and the trapping party headed back to the cabin. By the time they returned, only the horizon retained a bluish glow, but the temperature remained pleasant as Jupiter and Saturn appeared in the sky overhead.

"It's a nice night," Skeet said. "Good night to dine out. Taylor, you seem handy with a fire. Get one started in the pit while I instruct Jake in the fine art of cleaning a rabbit."

"Aw, no fair," Taylor said.

"Me?" Jake asked, looking at Skeet. "I've never cleaned anything except fish."

"Good time for you to learn. Besides, it's a two-handed job. Take the hare over to the chopping block while I get some knives."

Skeet fetched a small cleaver as well as a sharper knife with a thin blade, and brought them out to the chopping block—a pine stump located apart from the cabin. He also brought a kerosene lantern with him and hung it on a nearby branch.

"I do all my gutting and cleaning out here," he said. "Keeps the critters away from the cabin. So, let's get started. There're several ways to clean a rabbit—any animal, actually. Since we're all hungry, let's do it fast and dirty tonight. Pick up that cleaver and chop off its legs and head."

Jake looked down at the snowshoe hare. "Are you serious?"

"I am—unless you want to eat the head and the feet, that is. Just make sure you don't chop off any of your fingers while you do it. Small swings."

Jake picked up the cleaver and experimented with

positioning the hare the best way. Then he cut off the animal's front legs.

"Now the hind legs," Skeet said, watching him work. "Not all the way, just at the elbow joint there. Good. Now the head."

Jake's stomach lurched as he brought the blade down on the hare's neck. Even worse, the head didn't come off.

"You might need a couple of whacks there," Skeet explained. "Just keep your eyes on it and your left hand well clear."

With another two whacks, the hare's head rolled away from its body.

"Toss the head and the legs in that bucket there."

Jake followed his orders, then glanced over at Taylor, who already had a fire crackling. "Now what?"

"Gotta skin it," said Skeet. "Using the other knife, stretch out the skin at the base of the belly so you can pierce it without stabbing the meat or internal organs. Now slit it all the way up to the rabbit's neck. Once you've done that, just peel. That's it. One nice thing about rabbits is their skin peels away easily."

"I thought you said this was a hare," said Jake.

"Don't be a wise ass," Skeet said with a grin. "Time to get the guts out."

Following Skeet's instructions, Jake proceeded to remove the hare's internal organs. He thought he might throw up as he pulled the intestines out of the animal, but then he realized it wasn't that much different than gutting a fish—just a little messier and smellier. As a last step, Skeet had him remove the very hind end of the hare, where its bladder was still attached.

"Just throw that section away," he said. "Not worth messing with. Good. Now, all you gotta do is cut the hare up into pieces, and we're ready to make some stew."

While Jake chopped up carrots and potatoes, Skeet sent Taylor to a nearby stream with a flashlight to pull and wash some wild scallions. Jake fried the carrots and scallions in a pan and then tossed them into a larger pot with the potatoes, the rabbit, and a jar of home-canned tomatoes from the shelves in the cabin. Taylor hung the pot on an iron pole that Skeet had rigged over the fire pit.

"Now," said Skeet, "all we have to do is wait."

The boys pulled wooden chairs around the fire and sat down, one on either side of Skeet. Cody lay down at Taylor's feet and let out a big sigh. Skeet and the boys laughed, but Jake knew exactly how Cody was feeling. It felt good to let his guard down. Even though he and Taylor had only known Skeet for less than a day, Jake felt he could trust this man. Even better, Skeet had knowledge the boys needed.

Skeet seemed to be reading Jake's thoughts.

"So, boys," he said. "What's the story?"

"Well, uh, we kinda had some trouble back home," Jake said.

Skeet nodded. "Figured. And where was home?"

"Pittsburgh," Taylor blurted out.

To his credit, Skeet didn't press them on more details. Instead he said, "So what, you two thought you'd come out to the Wild West, live the life of mountain men?"

"Yeah, uh, something like that," said Jake.

Skeet mulled this over for a moment. "Well," he said, "don't take this the wrong way, boys, but I gotta tell you, it's a miracle you've lasted as long as you have. Your packs look fine for a day hike, but with what little gear you've got, you're lucky you haven't frozen or starved to death."

"We went to summer camp last year," Taylor said, "and were going to go again this year when—"

Jake cut him off, saying, "It's true we could use some help."

Skeet glanced at Taylor, then over at Jake. "Well, boys, since you saved my life, I got a proposal for you. You each have two good arms and I could use some help around here. How about you stick around for a couple of days while I teach you some basic survival skills?"

Jake quickly did some calculations in his head. He was eager to find his father, and the summer wasn't getting any longer.

But Skeet's right. Me and Taylor have been lucky so far. We need to know more to survive out here.

Taylor eagerly leaned forward in his chair. "Jake, that sounds good to me. Whaddya say?"

Jake nodded. "That would be okay."

"Good," Skeet said. "I gotta ask you a couple of questions

first, though. You're not in trouble with the law, are you?"

Jake was debating how to answer that, when Taylor said, "Shoot, no. We're not criminals."

"Good. The other thing . . . ," Skeet said. "Are your parents looking for you?"

"Mom's sick, in the hospital," Taylor said. "She probably doesn't even know we're gone."

Skeet thought some more. "Well, if we're going to do this, you have to let your mother know you're safe, okay?"

"We will," Jake assured him.

"Good. Now, it smells like that stew's about ready."

Taylor and Jake dished up food for themselves, Skeet, and Cody.

"Man, this is the best thing I've ever tasted!" Jake exclaimed, shoving a chunk of meat into his mouth.

Taylor said, "Jake, can you believe we're eatin' rabbit?"

"Hare," Jake corrected him.

"Maybe tomorrow we can start by teaching you how to build a deadfall trap so you can catch your own food."

"That'd be good," said Jake. "Only thing is, we'll probably be moving around a lot. We won't have time to just sit around and check our traps."

"Yeah," Taylor said before Jake could stop him. "We've gotta find Dad before fall—"

Taylor froze, realizing that he'd just given away their real purpose for being in Wyoming. Jake rolled his eyes and moaned. "Taylor . . ."

"Sorry, Jake," Taylor said, looking guilty.

Skeet stared at the boys. "You're looking for your father? Is that why you're out here?"

Jake sighed. "Yeah."

"Care to fill me in?"

"He came out here years ago," Taylor explained. "He wanted us to join him, but Mom didn't want to come. Then she got mixed up with her lousy boyfriend, Bull, who beats her up. That's why she's in the hospital, and that's why we came out here."

Skeet leaned forward in his chair. "Well, where is your dad now?"

"We don't know."

"He came out here looking for some kind of lost valley," Jake continued. "We have a letter from him saying that he found it, but he only gave us a few clues on how to find him."

Skeet stroked his salt-and-pepper beard as he stared into the fire. "This man. When did he first come out here?"

"Seven years ago," said Jake.

Skeet's black eyes suddenly darted toward Jake and bored into him.

Jake squirmed. "What? What is it?"

Skeet returned his gaze to the fire and leaned back in his chair. Finally he said, "Your father. I think I met him."

20

"What?" the boys shouted so loudly, Cody leaped to his feet.

"Where? When did you see him?" Taylor demanded.

"Now, don't get too excited," Skeet said. "It was a long time ago. Over the years, I've met plenty of crackpots around here. A lot of 'em come to Wyoming looking for just the kind of paradise your father talked about. And most of 'em didn't know an ax from a baton.

"About six, seven years ago, though, I was tracking wolves up near Yellowstone. I was following a small pack ten miles from the nearest trail, when I ran into this guy. We camped together one night, and after dinner he started talking about his family back east somewhere and this lost valley he was searching for. To be honest, I didn't put much stock in it, but this guy seemed to know a lot about the outdoors, and I enjoyed his company. The next morning we parted ways and I never saw him again."

"But," Jake said, "you said you've met a lot of people out here looking for paradise or something like that. How do you know it was our father?"

Skeet took his gaze from the fire. "Because," he said, "your names—Jake and Taylor—I knew that combo sounded familiar. He talked about you two."

"Wh-whoa!" Taylor sputtered. "Can you help us find him?"

Skeet shook his head. "I hate to say it, but probably not. This is big country, and finding your father would be like finding a shotgun pellet on a beach. You said he left you some clues?"

"In a letter," Jake said.

"Well, then, you've probably got a better idea of where to look than I do."

Taylor jumped to his feet. "Jake, we have to get out of here and keep looking! Dad's close! I know he is!"

Skeet held up his good hand. "Now, just a minute, fellas. I want you to find your dad. But like I said before, you're lucky you even made it this far. You need to prepare. How about a deal: you promise to stick around for a few days—long enough so I can teach you a few more survival skills and get you set up properly—then I'll take you wherever you want to go."

"Jake, what do you think?" Taylor asked.

The thought of finding their father set Jake's heart pounding.

But Skeet's right. We need to be better prepared. Smarter. Also, maybe Skeet will think of a way to figure out where Dad is.

"Okay, deal," Jake said to Skeet. "We'll stay a week. Then you'll help point us in the right direction."

Skeet's face relaxed. "Good. We'll start tomorrow."

Skeet's training began before dawn the next day, when he took the boys out to set deadfall traps. He also showed them how to set snare traps, but again he warned against using them unless the boys' lives depended on it.

They returned to camp as a faint but brilliant dawn spread across the sky.

"Now," Skeet said, "while we're waiting to see if we catch anything in the traps, we got a lot of other things to cover. You boys said you'll be moving around a lot, so traps won't always meet your needs. You said you'd caught some trout . . . ?"

Jake explained their fish trap and improvised net, and Skeet nodded approvingly. "I'm impressed. But next we've got to get you boys set up for some hunting."

Skeet showed the boys how to make primitive slingshots and bows. The slingshots proved relatively easy to manufacture—basically cut-off forked branches with lengths of surgical tubing Skeet had on hand.

"Making a bow is harder," Skeet told them. "To make a proper bow, you have to cut the right length of wood, shape it, and dry it—a process that can take weeks or months. You haven't got time for that."

Instead Skeet showed them how to cut a fresh five-foot-long sapling about two inches in diameter. "Stay away from pine, poplar, and willow trees," he told them. "Those'll usually break. But almost anything else that's strong and springy will work."

The boys cut their own bows and strung them using some elk sinew cord Skeet had made. Skeet gave them a couple of factory-made arrows to test out their new weapons, and in no time, Taylor could hit a paper-plate target from twenty-five feet away. Jake struggled, sending most of his arrows well wide of the target.

Seeing Jake's frustration, Skeet put his hand on the older boy's shoulder. "Don't be hard on yourself. We all have different talents. It takes brains and brawn to survive out here. Never forget that patience and practice are the most important survival tools."

Over the next few days, Skeet continued preparing the boys for living in the wilderness. He gave them each larger backpacks to carry, and a variety of extra equipment, including a pot and frying pan, a rain tarp, a trenching tool, and a couple of old musty sleeping bags. He showed them different ways of making shelters to live under, and how to start a fire using a magnesium flint. Mostly, he showed them how to find and follow game, and work on perfecting their hunting skills.

After three days Taylor could hit a paper plate from forty feet away with his bow or slingshot, and had already killed some squirrels and a snowshoe hare. Jake still struggled. However, on the fourth day, Jake and Cody got up early to check on some deadfall traps when Cody suddenly froze. Jake followed the dog's gaze. About fifteen feet away, he spotted a gray bird almost perfectly camouflaged under a sage bush. Jake wasn't sure what the bird was, but it looked like some kind of wild chicken.

Slowly, Jake removed his bow from his shoulder and pulled an arrow from a quiver Skeet had shown him how to make. He nocked the arrow, pulled back the string, aimed, and fired.

A spray of feathers flew from the bird, and at first Jake felt sure he'd missed his shot again. As he and Cody sprinted forward, though, Jake saw the bird pinned to the ground, the arrow piercing its chest. Cody barked, and Jake grinned.

"Sorry, bird," he muttered, kneeling next to the dead animal. "But thank you."

Jake and Cody carried the bird triumphantly back to the cabin, and seeing it, Skeet and Taylor both whooped.

"Whoa! Way to go, brother!" Taylor exclaimed.

"Nice blue grouse," Skeet said, admiring the bird. "How you going to cook her?"

Jake had been pondering that on the way back to the cabin. "I was thinking about roasting it over some coals—you know, like those rotisserie things in the grocery stores."

Skeet's eyebrows scrunched, and he nodded. "Yep, that'd work. You'll lose most of the juices and a lot of the nutrients, though. You feel like learning a tastier method?"

"Sure."

"Okay, but first, you gotta clean her."

It took Jake what felt like an age to remove the hundreds of dense feathers covering the animal. After opening up and rinsing out the bird, Skeet showed the boys how to dig a pit about two feet square and eighteen inches deep. The boys lined the pit with flat rocks and then built a fire down in it. When the rocks glowed red-hot, Skeet instructed them to scrape out the fire and coals, and line the bottom with grass. Onto this grass bed, they laid the grouse, some root vegetables, and two squirrels Taylor had killed with his slingshot.

"Now add another layer of grass and cover that all up with dirt," said Skeet.

"But there's no fire," Taylor objected. "How's it going to cook?"

"The heat from the rocks will cook it slowly, but we gotta leave it for a few hours."

Jake was skeptical, but while the food cooked, Skeet suggested that they practice making arrows to pass the time, now that they had plenty of feathers.

Two days earlier, the boys had cut some straight alder shoots, each about two feet long. Now they used their pocketknives to whittle the ends of the shoots into sharp points and cut nocks into the opposite ends. They hardened the shafts—especially the points—in the coals of the fire they'd used to boil water. When they'd done that, they selected the best tail feathers from the grouse, peeled the barbs from one side of each shaft, and glued three of the shafts to the nock end of each arrow.

"If you don't have any glue, you can also use tree sap," Skeet told them.

Taylor hurried to try out the new arrows. He hung a plate from a string about twenty feet away and let three of the arrows fly. The first two missed, but he impaled the plate with the third arrow.

"They don't fly as straight as the store-bought ones," he said, "but they're better than I thought."

By the time they finished archery practice, it was time to check the meat. Jake scraped away the soil and grass layer to reveal their meal. The rich scents of the wild game, potatoes, and carrots filled the air.

"Oh, man, that smells good!" Taylor enthused. "Let's eat!"

The meal proved to be as delicious as it smelled. The blue grouse tasted a bit like chicken, but richer and more flavorful.

"I think this is the best food I've ever eaten," Jake said.

"That's, like, the third time you've said that in the past week." Taylor laughed.

"That's because it's true!"

Skeet grinned. "That's because you caught it and cooked it yourself. Nothin' else like it, is there?"

The boys nodded.

As it began to grow dark, Skeet lit a couple of kerosene lanterns, and the boys went into the cabin for their next lesson—sewing. By now, the boys had collected enough furs that they could make some primitive protection from the elements, and Skeet even taught them a bit of hand-stitching. After about an hour, though, Taylor had had enough, and announced he was off to stretch his legs. Jake watched him go. He'd noticed that his brother had been acting jumpy all day, but he hadn't thought much of it.

Probably just impatient to get looking for Dad, he thought. Even though Jake felt much better prepared for the wild after their time with Skeet, he knew they'd have to get going soon.

Jake busied himself stitching together two rabbit pelts, until he realized that Taylor had been gone for ages, and it was seriously dark outside. Putting his things to one side, he went out to check on his brother.

Skeet grunted, busily bent over his wolverine notebooks and maps at the wooden table, while Cody happily gnawed on an old elk leg bone.

Jake left the cabin, closing the door behind him, and walked to the outhouse.

"Hello?" he called, but the outhouse was empty. Jake stood under the night sky, perplexed. Then he thought he heard a voice up the hill. He climbed toward it, and as he approached, he could see the silhouette of his brother against the night sky above him. It sounded like Taylor was talking to someone.

That's weird, Jake thought. *Is he talking to himself?*

As he drew closer, however, Jake saw Taylor holding their cell phone—the one Jake had taken from the drawer back in Pennsylvania.

"Taylor, what are you doing?" Jake exclaimed, rushing up and wresting the phone from him. He quickly punched the phone's end button.

"I wasn't doing anything," Taylor said defensively.

"Who were you talking to?" Jake demanded.

"I, uh . . ."

"Did you call Pennsylvania? Did you tell anyone where we are?" Jake's pulse pounded in his ears.

"No! Course not! I was just trying to call the hospital to find out if Mom's okay! I've been worried about her, Jake."

"What did they say?" Jake asked. He was still angry, but more than that he suddenly needed to know.

"I don't know, but I don't think she's in the hospital anymore."

Jake let out an exasperated sigh. "Taylor, how could you be so stupid? If they trace this call, the police will know exactly where we are. Maybe even Bull will find out!"

"But it's one of those disposable phones, isn't it? They can't trace those, can they?"

"Taylor, I don't know, but if you keep doing things without thinking, we're going to end up back in Pittsburgh and we'll never find Dad!"

Now Taylor got angry. "Maybe that's true, Jake, but you don't even seem to care about Mom. She could still be hurt. She might even be dead for all we know, and you don't care! Sometimes you're as bad as Bull!"

With that, a new surge of anger filled Jake. Didn't Taylor realize how much pressure he was under to take care of everyone? Of course he cared about Mom. He was just doing what he thought was best. He lifted up the phone and dashed it against a nearby granite rock, shattering it into a dozen pieces.

Taylor and Jake just stared at each other. Even in the starlight, their eyes blazed.

"Now who's being the idiot?" Taylor brushed past his brother and started back down the mountain. "I'm done taking orders from you, Jake. I'm going to find Dad on my own!"

21

Jake stormed back to the cabin, furious with his brother. *How could he be so stupid?* he thought. *It's like he wants us to get caught!* But as he replayed the conversation in his head, something struck a chord. Taylor's words about being like Bull echoed in his skull. Why had he thrown the phone against the rocks? Losing his temper like that *was* just like Bull.

By the time Jake reached the cabin door, his anger had been replaced by guilt—and worry. He was meant to look after Taylor; they were meant to stick together.

As Jake pushed through the cabin door, Skeet looked up in surprise.

"Did Taylor come back?" Jake asked, glancing around the small room.

"He did," said Skeet. "He rushed in here and grabbed his old day pack and said he wanted to show you something. Isn't he with you?"

For a moment Jake didn't answer, the gears spinning in his head. Then he said, "He was, but . . ."

Now Skeet pushed his chair back from the table. "He what?"

"We had a fight. I . . . said some things I shouldn't have, and Taylor said he was going to go look for our dad by himself."

Skeet stood now, concern deepening the lines on his face. "Do you think that's what he did?"

"Maybe. I don't know. I need to go look for him."

Jake reached for his own pack, but Skeet held up his hand. "Now hold on. Let's think this through, Jake. Has Taylor ever run off like this before?"

"Well, yeah. Sometimes, back in Pennsylvania," Jake remembered.

"And did he always come back?" Skeet asked.

"After a while," Jake admitted.

"So maybe he just needs time."

"We haven't got time—we've got to go look for him now!" Jake cried.

"Okay, okay," Skeet said. "I just thought it might be safer to wait than rush off into the dark, but you're right. We can go; but we have to be prepared!"

Jake knew Skeet was right, so he quickly began preparing

his pack. Besides food, he filled it with the items Skeet had given him, including matches and the magnesium fire starter, a trenching tool, a cooking pot, a first aid kit, their father's journal, a rain tarp, and one of the sleeping bags. Jake also slung his bow and quiver over his shoulder, and stuffed the slingshot into his pack.

"Can that dog of yours do any tracking?" Skeet asked. "His nose might be a lot better than your eyes."

Jake looked down at Cody. "I think so."

Skeet handed him one of Taylor's shirts. "Take this. It might help Cody key in on Taylor's scent. While you look for him, I'll keep an eye out around here. I'll cover all the places we set traps and look for any other signs. If you don't find him by tomorrow, you better get back here so we can launch a real search party."

Jake let out a deep breath. "Okay."

Skeet patted him on the shoulder. "Don't waste energy worrying. That'll only tire you out. And remember, there's still a good chance he'll come back on his own—another reason for you to check back in here tomorrow."

"Okay. Thanks."

Jake and Cody left the cabin right as the dark shades of night began to soften. Jake squatted down next to Cody and held the shirt to the dog's nose.

"Cody, go find Taylor."

The dog seemed to understand. He began rushing around the ground near the cabin.

Taylor's scent must be everywhere around here, Jake realized. After just a minute, though, Cody barked and began heading north, away from the cabin.

"Good dog, Cody," Jake told him, hurrying to catch up.

Sweeping the ground with his torch, Jake could just make out some footprints, and he knelt down beside them. Jake was no expert, but Skeet had taught him a few clues for telling how old a track might be, and these seemed like they could be Taylor's.

"These look pretty fresh," Jake muttered. The edges of the prints were still sharp.

Cody looked back at Jake impatiently, and the two continued, climbing over mountain ridges and down into rugged valleys.

Where was Taylor going? Jake wondered. He guessed his brother had gotten turned around or lost, but he also thought maybe Taylor had something else in mind that he hadn't told Jake about. Every once in a while Jake thought he and Cody had lost the trail, but the terrier rarely waivered, and sure enough Jake would soon find new tracks.

When the sun had climbed halfway up into the sky, Jake and Cody found a makeshift lean-to with a fresh bed of pine needles under it. They paused to examine it, and Jake felt sure it was Taylor's work. Jake sat down only long enough for a drink of water and to give Cody a piece of Skeet's elk jerky, before carrying on their search.

Soon Jake and Cody were on a kind of game trail going farther into the mountains. Jake made his way across the rocky land when suddenly both he and Cody froze. Up ahead, they heard a terrible whining cry like a banshee. The cry continued, rising and falling in pitch, and then it was followed by a deep growl.

Jake shivered. "Stay!" he ordered Cody, and for one of the only times in his life, Cody looked happy to stop.

Jake quickly unslung his bow and nocked an arrow. Then he walked past Cody and moved carefully forward.

The cry continued, and then Jake heard a terrified human voice call: "Get back!"

"Taylor!" Jake yelled, and ran forward, the bow still in his hands. Cody followed him, barking furiously.

They came upon a scene out of a bad dream. Thirty feet away, Taylor sat trapped halfway back into a ten-foot-deep cave. At the far end of the cave cowered a bobcat kitten about the size of a housecat, but at the mouth of the cave snarled a full-grown mama bobcat.

Jake immediately sized up the situation.

Taylor's trapped between the mother and her kitten!

"Taylor, get out of there!" Jake shouted.

"I can't, Jake. My leg!"

Jake saw blood oozing from Taylor's ripped-open pant leg and realized that his brother couldn't move. Cody growled and barked but stayed well away from the snarling cat.

"Go away!" Taylor shouted at the mother bobcat, this time throwing a rock from the cave floor at the snarling animal. The bobcat barely flinched.

Jake drew his bow and took aim. The mother cat turned her head and snarled at him, but she didn't give up her position. Jake lowered his bow, realizing that with his poor aim, he'd probably shoot his brother instead of the bobcat.

"Jake, do something!" Taylor shouted.

Quickly dropping his pack, Jake pulled out his home-made slingshot. He selected a white piece of quartzite, drew back the surgical cord, and aimed. The rock flew with a hiss, striking the bobcat's flank. Crying out, the cat leaped and spun to face Jake and Cody directly. For an instant Jake thought the cat would attack, but Cody seemed to have found his courage and now stood barking fiercely between Jake and the cat.

Jake picked up another rock and fired. This time he hit the bobcat squarely on the nose. The cat shrieked, and in the turmoil, the bobcat kitten streaked past Taylor, out of the cave, and up the rocky slope. The mother saw her kitten make its getaway, screamed at Jake one last time, and then turned to follow her young.

Jake rushed to his brother.

"Taylor, what happened? How badly are you hurt?"

With his brother there, Taylor burst into sobs. "Jake, I'm sorry! I was such an idiot for leaving!"

Jake hugged him. "No, it was my fault," he said. "I shouldn't have yelled at you. You were right to try to find out about Mom."

He pulled himself away from Taylor's arms to examine the wound on his leg. "Did the bobcat do this?"

"Yeah," Taylor said, snot running from his nose. "I . . . I crawled into the cave and didn't see the baby in the back. I was trying to chase it out of the cave when the mother came back and attacked me. I held her off with rocks for a while, but she was about to attack again when you and Cody came."

Jake studied the wound. The bobcat had clawed Taylor's calf, and the blood flowed freely. The wound looked angry, and the leg had already swollen, showing signs of infection. Taylor's face was as pale as the quartzite that littered the cave floor.

Jake gave Taylor a drink of water and then had him lie back on his pack. Taylor winced as Jake rinsed out the wound with fresh water and, using gauze from the first aid kit, tied a pressure band over the wound. He considered tying a tourniquet, but remembered that they should only be used to stop extreme bleeding.

"I don't feel so good, Jake."

Besides being pale, Taylor had started sweating profusely. *That wound's infected for sure,* Jake thought to himself.

"Do you think you can walk?"

"I . . . I don't think so."

Jake pondered his options. He rechecked the first aid

kit, and though it held bandages, gauze, and a small tube of antibiotic, he didn't see anything that would help Taylor right now. Next he turned to their father's journal. Abe had reserved a whole section of it for notes on useful medicinal plants, and Jake had read it over many times. Skimming quickly through the pages, he spotted several plants that might help his brother.

He gripped Taylor's hand again. "Listen," he said. "I'll get you settled, but then I have to go find us a couple of things. I promise I'll be back quickly, though, okay?"

Taylor nodded weakly, unable to argue.

Jake unrolled the sleeping bag he'd brought. He unzipped it and spread it wide like a blanket, then helped Taylor scoot over on top of it.

He told Cody, "You stay with Taylor," but the terrier had already curled up protectively next to Taylor on the sleeping bag.

Jake emptied Taylor's day pack and stuffed their father's journal and the trenching tool inside. Then he set out toward a pine-covered hilltop a quarter of a mile away.

Jake wasn't sure what he would find, but along the trail he spotted several yarrow plants, with wispy grayish leaves and constellations of tightly spaced white flowers. He flipped through his dad's journal to make sure he was remembering correctly, and then he tore out several of the plants and stuffed them into Taylor's day pack.

Reaching the pine-covered hilltop, he again pulled out

the journal, looking for other plants that might help. At first he didn't see much. Then he stopped and examined a low-growing prickly leaved plant with green berries on it. He was pretty sure he remembered it, but he checked the journal again to make sure.

"Oregon grape," he said. "Bingo."

Pulling out the trenching tool, he began digging up several of the plants, cutting off and saving their yellow roots. When he had collected about a pound of them, he hurried back to the cave.

When he got there, Taylor looked even worse. The bleeding on his leg wound had stopped, but had begun to crust over, and the flesh around it looked red and inflamed. Taylor moaned softly, but he didn't seem fully conscious.

Jake built a small fire at the entrance to the cave, filled the small pot with the last of the water he'd brought, and set the pot at the edge of the flames. He pulled out the yarrow plants and began crushing them into a paste that he placed on some gauze from the first aid kit. When the water had almost boiled, he poured some of it over the gauze to form a kind of warm poultice that he placed directly onto Taylor's wound.

Taylor sat up and yelled with pain.

"It's okay! It's okay!" Jake soothed. "I'm just putting some medicine on your wound. Lie back down."

When he and Cody had gotten Taylor settled again, Jake crushed up the Oregon grape roots and added them to the rest of the hot water in the pot. He let the mixture steep and then strained the tealike mixture into the metal cup Skeet had given him.

When it had cooled, Jake tried a little of the drink himself. The tea tasted bitter, but medicinal somehow, and he took it over to Taylor. Jake put his arm under his brother's back and helped him into a sitting position.

"Here, Taylor, drink this."

Taylor didn't seem to know where he was, but his lips parted when Jake pressed the cup against them. His father's journal had said to use the mixture sparingly, so Jake gave his brother only three or four sips and saved the rest for later. Then he lay Taylor back down and zipped him up in the sleeping bag.

Jake wasn't sure what the medicines would do—if they would do anything at all.

I should still probably go back and get Skeet, he thought—but he didn't dare leave his brother right now. This wasn't what was supposed to happen when they left Pittsburgh to find their father. Jake was supposed to be making them safer, not putting them in even more danger. Exhausted from being up for more than twenty-four hours straight, Jake used his backpack as a pillow and lay down next to Taylor and Cody.

Please let Taylor be all right. Please! he prayed as he drifted off into an uneasy sleep.

22

The next morning Jake woke to Taylor's moans. While the light was just beginning to creep over the horizon, he decided he'd better refill their empty water bottles and the cooking pot. He rebuilt the small fire outside of the cave and then turned to Cody.

"You keep standing guard," Jake said. The terrier seemed to understand, and he didn't budge from Taylor's side.

Jake had to hike more than a mile back to a stream he'd crossed earlier. Along the way he stayed alert for signs of the bobcat, but he saw only a small group of elk a quarter mile off the sheep trail. After refilling their water bottles and the cooking pot, he returned to Taylor's side.

His heart pounding, he laid his hand on Taylor's forehead. To his relief, the skin felt cool from the morning mountain air, and no longer burned with fever. Jake bent over to listen to his brother's now regular breathing.

Thank you! Thank you! he prayed, though not sure exactly to whom. He also thanked the world for his dad's journal—without it, the situation could have been deadly.

Jake set about building a new fire and was feeding a dead pine bough onto it when he heard Taylor weakly call, "Jake?"

He turned to his brother. "Taylor, how are you feeling?"

"Hungry."

Jake laughed.

"Is it morning?" Taylor asked. "Did the bobcat come back?"

"Yes—and no. You had a fever most of the night, but you look better now. Let me help you sit up."

Jake helped Taylor into a sitting position.

"I feel woozy. What's this on my leg?" he asked, reaching down to the poultice.

"Some medicine—from yarrow plants."

"You did this?"

"Yeah. Now just relax while I make us some food."

Jake made Taylor drink more of the cold Oregon grape concoction, then boiled more water and stirred in a seven-grain cereal mixture Skeet had given him. Jake watched with relief as Taylor bolted down the meal, and afterward Jake helped his brother stand up.

"Do you think you can walk?"

Taylor took a couple of shaky steps.

"Just about," Taylor said, grabbing on to Jake's arm.

"Awesome," Jake said. "In that case, we should get back to Skeet before he sends out a search party!"

Jake cleaned up their camp, and the boys slowly set out back along the sheep trail. They reached the cabin just before noon, and they were surprised to find Skeet missing. Fifteen minutes later, though, they heard the Green Monster rumble up the mountain track. Jake and Cody went out to greet him.

"Did you find Taylor?" Skeet asked, leaping out of the truck.

"Yeah. He's inside resting on your bunk," Jake said, explaining what had happened.

Skeet clapped him on the back. "I think you've got the makings of a first-class mountain man, Jake—or medicine man, at least. Let's go take a look at him."

Skeet and Taylor went inside, where Skeet carefully removed the poultice from Taylor's leg to take a look. "You did a nice job with this, Jake. Still, I think we ought to run Taylor down to the clinic in town, maybe get him some antibiotics and have them clean out the wound properly."

Jake and Taylor nodded.

"Also, I may have some good news for you," Skeet added.

"What's that?" Taylor asked, sitting up on Skeet's bed.

"Well, I ran into town this morning for a few supplies, and also wanted to see if anyone might be looking for you boys. Stopped by a friend of mine at the park ranger office."

"You didn't tell him about us, did you?" Jake asked, alarmed.

"Now, calm down. No, I didn't. I just told him I was there to say hello and asked if he'd been busy lately. However, it wasn't two minutes before he told me they were looking for two boys and a dog, and that apparently, someone had dropped by saying there was some news about their mother."

"Mom!" Taylor shouted, his eyes darting to Jake.

Despite his brother's enthusiasm, Jake saw red flags. "How did he know that?"

"I don't really know," Skeet answered. "I imagine he got some kinda alert through a social services agency, or maybe it came through the police."

"What does it matter, Jake?" Taylor said, lowering his feet to the floor. "Maybe Mom's okay. Maybe we can get her to come out and join us once we find Dad!"

"I don't know. . . ."

Cody jumped up next to Taylor and did a little dance, sensing excitement in the room.

"What's not to know?" Taylor pressed. "Maybe Mom's looking for us."

"Taylor," Jake said. "It could be a trap. What if they just want to catch us and send us back to Pennsylvania?"

Taylor turned to Skeet. "Do you think it's a trap?"

Skeet stroked his beard. "This isn't my area of expertise," he answered. "But I think it might be worth checking out. I could drive you into town for a look around. If things seem sketchy, we can skedaddle on outta there."

"Jake, c'mon!" Taylor pleaded.

Jake's stomach clenched, but he also still felt guilty about his fight with his brother the day before.

Reluctantly, he nodded. "Okay, but we have to be careful."

Taylor stood up and hugged his brother. "It's going to be all right. You'll see!"

After the boys packed up their things, Skeet drove them and Cody into town. He parked at a diner at the far end of the small street of businesses. "Okay," he said. "The rangers' office is right down the street, past that motel. I'll grab some coffee in here while you boys check it out."

"Can Cody stay with you?" Jake asked. "It might attract more attention if he's with us."

"Sure," said Skeet. "Cody and me'll come back and wait in the Green Monster. Afterward, we'll run Taylor by that clinic, make sure his leg is okay."

"Thanks," Jake said.

The boys left their large packs with Skeet, but Jake took the day pack that held their dad's journal, Bull's cash, and a couple of other items. Jake felt his heart beat faster as they made their way down the sidewalk. He didn't like that someone was looking for them—the authorities, at that—but they had to find out about their mom; Taylor had been right.

"How we gonna do this?" Taylor asked as they continued down the sidewalk toward the rangers' office.

"I should probably go in by myself," Jake said. "You stay outside, and if anything happens, run back to Skeet."

"Or maybe I should just go in with you?"

"Well . . . ," Jake began as they approached the motel Skeet had pointed out. "That's probably a good idea, except . . ."

"Except what?"

But before Jake had time to answer, he spotted a black truck parked on the corner, set back from the main road. Jake froze, and a wave of nausea washed through him. He recognized the truck; he would have recognized it anywhere. But he couldn't believe it. It didn't matter now that they were hundreds of miles away from home; he'd found them.

It was a trap! Jake screamed inside his head, watching as the stocky surly figure of the man they thought they'd left behind forever stormed out of the truck and slammed the door behind him.

"Bull!" Taylor said, and gasped, grabbing Jake's arm.

"Quick, Taylor, run!" Jake shouted, springing into action, already turning away.

"Jake, I can't!" Taylor cried, and in the next instant, Bull fell upon them. Rushing around the truck's bumper, Bull grabbed the boys by their arms, practically growling with anger.

"Well, look who we have here!" he sneered.

"No! Get off of us!" Taylor cried, trying to wriggle his arm out of Bull's clutches. But it was no use. Before Jake or Taylor could react, Bull hustled them to one of the nearby motel rooms, pushed open the door, and threw the boys onto the bed, slamming the door behind him.

"How considerate of you boys to show up," Bull said, leering over them. "And to think, I just happened to book me a room right here. Gotta say, fortune favors the well-prepared."

"What are you doing here?" Taylor said, gasping, unable to believe who was standing in front of him.

The grin on Bull's face turned mean. "What do you think I'm doing here, you little snots? Once I realized you'd taken my cash and run away, it wasn't all that hard to follow you. You left clues across half the country—your picture is up everywhere. And lucky ol' me is the one to find you . . . and now I want my reward."

"What are you talking about?" Jake cried.

"You got a big chunk of money of mine, and I want it back—*now*!"

"You can't do anything to us—we know you shot that guy!" Taylor told him. "The rangers' office already knows we're here and the rangers are looking for us—we'll tell them everything!"

Bull laughed. "Oh, please. Just who do you think talked to them in the first place? I knew you'd come crawling out of the woodwork once I mentioned your *mommy*."

Jake groaned inside, his worst fears realized.

"Where is she?" Jake asked.

"You beat her up, didn't you?" Taylor demanded.

Bull scoffed. "What do *you* think? And if you don't give me my dough, I'm gonna do a lot worse to you."

Bull reached for Jake's day pack, but Jake ripped it away. As he did so, the zipper on the pack tore open, and a few pages from their father's journal fell to the floor, including the letters to their mom. Jake sprang to the far side of the bed.

"What's this?" Bull laughed. "Moose Island? Wildflower Waterfall? Your dad really was a crackpot!"

"Stay away from us, Bull!" Jake shouted.

"Enough of this crap," Bull growled as he pulled out the pistol the boys remembered all too well, and pointed it directly at Jake. Taylor scooted back, shielding his brother.

"Leave him alone, Bull!" Taylor shouted.

"I'll shoot both of you right now if you don't hand over that pack. I need that money!" Bull demanded.

Giving Bull's money back was the last thing Jake wanted to do, but he also knew he and Taylor were trapped. He unzipped the pack the rest of the way and removed the large Ziploc bag containing the money. Leaving the pack on the bed, he stepped around the end of it and handed the bag to Bull.

Bull's eyes gleamed as he took the money.

"You got what you want," said Jake. "Now leave us and Mom alone!"

Bull sneered. "Oh, I've got the money. But you brats and me still got some unfinished business."

Bull raised the revolver, preparing to strike Jake in the face with the gun. As Bull's arm began to swing, however, Jake heard a slapping sound and something sing through the air.

Bull cried out, dropping the gun and clutching the side of his face. Jake's head whipped around to see Taylor holding Jake's slingshot in his hand.

Bull bellowed and doubled over in pain, blood dripping through his fingers. Without thinking, Jake ripped a table lamp out of the wall socket and raised it high in the air before bringing it down hard over Bull's head. The big man collapsed onto the floor with a sickening thud.

Jake stared in horror at the scene. The man he'd feared for so long was laid out in front of him, crimson drops beginning to stain the shabby motel carpet.

"Oh my God," he muttered.

"Quick, Jake, we have to go," Taylor cried, tugging at Jake. But Jake, letting the lamp slip from his fingers, was rooted to the spot.

"I'm serious, Jake," Taylor cried. "We have to move *now!*"

Jake just stared, wide-eyed. *What have I done?*

23

Taylor grabbed the Ziploc bag full of money back from Bull and stuffed it into his pack. More pages and letters flew from his father's journal, landing on the floor— he scooped them up and shoved them in too.

"C'mon!" he said again to Jake.

"Is he dead?" Jake asked, staring down at Bull.

"I don't know—and I don't want to find out! We gotta go!"

All the color had drained from Jake's face, but the sight of Taylor bustling into action snapped him back to reality. They couldn't hang around here. Not now.

Grabbing their things, Jake and Taylor raced through the motel room door, leaving Bull and his black truck behind.

As they ran back up the street, checking behind them as they went, they saw Skeet up ahead emerging from the

Green Monster. Even from a distance, they could tell he had a worried frown on his face.

"You boys okay? What happened?"

"We need to get out of here." Jake gulped, desperately trying to look less flustered than he felt.

"Why, what—" Skeet began, but Jake just cut him off.

"Now!"

They all piled into the truck, and Skeet headed directly out of town. As they drove, Skeet asked what happened.

Jake stalled. "They didn't know anything about our mom."

"What *did* they say? Why are you so worked up?" Skeet continued. Jake felt like his mind was going into overdrive— the image of Bull on the floor of the motel room just kept on coming back to him, and he was beginning to break out in a cold sweat.

Taylor kept quiet and looked anxiously up at Jake, but Jake remained in a kind of trance, staring out the window.

Skeet nodded. "Fine—if that's how you want it. Maybe I should just drop you off at the police station—let them take care of you."

"No!" Taylor said. "We've got to find our dad. If we go to the police, we'll never find him."

"Boys, I don't know. . . ." Skeet said.

"Taylor's right," said Jake, suddenly frantic. "Skeet, please, we've come this far! *Please.* You have to help us!"

Skeet continued driving. "Do you even know where to look?"

"Not exactly." Jake fumbled his words. "But at the cabin, I studied my dad's notes and your maps, and I think I narrowed it down."

Jake told him what he'd figured out, while Skeet mulled it over. "Well, that's a pretty well-known spot, but it's not easy getting there. There's no way to drive to it."

"Can you get us close?"

Skeet stroked his beard. "Yeah, boys. I think I can."

Skeet drove the boys back into Grand Teton National Park. As they drove through the tiny town of Moose, Taylor suddenly exclaimed, "Jake, wait a minute. This town is called Moose. Could this be what Dad was talking about in his journal?"

"Possibly," Jake said, "but I think maybe Dad had another moose in mind."

Skeet continued driving to Moran Junction and then turned left. Instead of driving on to Yellowstone National Park, however, Skeet turned onto a smaller road that led them to a tiny boat dock. In a small bay, a couple of dozen boats had been anchored in the calm waters of Jackson Lake. Skeet parked and turned off the truck.

"What are we doing *here*?" Taylor asked.

"Well," Skeet answered, "look all the way across the lake. You see that steep valley?"

"Yeah."

"That's called Waterfalls Canyon. If you look carefully, you'll see two steep waterfalls. They don't look like much from here, but each one of them is more than two hundred feet high."

Taylor looked at Jake. "Is one of them the waterfall Dad mentioned in his letter, Jake? How do you know?"

Jake pointed to a small low island less than half a mile offshore. "Because that's Moose Island."

Taylor grinned. "How'd you find it?"

"I didn't until I starting looking at Skeet's maps. Then I saw that the island and the waterfalls lined up with the clues in the letter. To find directions to his hidden valley, he said to look west across the moose's neck to where the wildflower falls."

"Those waterfalls are called Wildflower Falls?" Taylor asked, confused.

"Columbine Cascade," Skeet clarified. "Columbine is a kind of wildflower."

"Ah . . ." Taylor understood. "But, Jake, those falls are on the other side of the lake. How are we going to get over there?"

"Leave that to me," Skeet said, climbing out of the truck. "Grab your stuff."

The boys and Cody followed Skeet to a small marina building. Next to it lay a long shape under a tarp. Skeet removed the tarp to reveal a beautiful forest-green fiberglass canoe with two paddles.

"This is yours?" Jake asked.

"Yep. The guys who run the marina let me keep it here

during the summer. It saves me a lot of walking to get around the lake. Figured it might do the same for you."

"You're going to let us take it?" Taylor asked.

Skeet grinned. "Well, you gotta bring it back if you can. Otherwise, pull it up onshore on the other side, and I'll fetch it later. It's about three miles to the other side. I figure if you paddle hard, you can make it across the lake in about an hour—unless the wind comes up. Then all bets are off."

"There's no wind," Taylor observed. "We won't have any trouble."

"Don't be too sure," Skeet warned. "I've seen boats capsize on this lake. Now, hurry up!"

The boys carried the canoe down to the water's edge, placed their packs in the bottom, and strapped on the life jackets left in the boat.

"Hop in!" Taylor told Cody, and the dog leaped into the canoe.

Before they climbed in, they each shook Skeet's hand. "Thanks for all your help," Jake said. Despite the turmoil he was in, he knew that they couldn't have gotten this far without Skeet's help—they'd learned so much from him. It would be hard work going into the unknown without him.

"Yeah," said Taylor. "You saved us."

Skeet grinned. "Just returning the favor, boys. Now go on and get out of here!" With his good arm, Skeet helped push them away from the shore, and without looking back, the boys began paddling.

Cutting between Cow Island and the north tip of Moose Island, the boys headed out into open water, making a bee-line for Waterfalls Canyon on the far side of the lake. Cody stood with his paws at the edge of the canoe, as if he were the captain of a ship.

Jake provided the steering and most of the power while Taylor added what manpower he could, and they quickly covered the first mile or so. *We'll be there in no time*, Jake thought.

Then, suddenly, the wind swept down from the north. To keep from being carried all the way to the south end of the lake, the boys had to point the canoe northwest and paddle hard into the gusts.

"Oh man," said Taylor, quickly tiring. "Skeet was right about the wind. This is brutal."

Jake didn't even grunt; he just strained hard against his paddle. The struggle was a relief from the thoughts whirling around in his mind. One moment he was back in the motel room with Bull, replaying over and over what had happened. The next moment he was struggling with the paddles, water splashing into his face and clouding his vision. He kept telling himself that he had to do it—it was self-defense. *Right?* But would the cops see it that way? What if he'd killed Bull? He would be a monster—just like him.

The wind continued to buffet the canoe, pushing it

like a sail. Soon Jake's arms and back burned from effort. It took the boys what felt like hours to cover the distance across the lake. Finally, though, the longed-for shoreline came into view. Hopping out of the boat, they felt the rocky lake bed beneath their feet and managed to hoist the canoe up and onto the shore, collapsing in exhaustion next to the boat.

"Oh man, that was rough," Taylor said, groaning.

"No kidding," Jake replied.

After recovering their strength, the boys hid Skeet's canoe among some pine trees and, reluctantly, hoisted their packs.

"How are you feeling?" Jake asked.

"My leg's okay," said Taylor. "I just don't have any energy. It's like it's been drained out of me."

"Do you want to stay here while I go look for some clues?" Jake asked.

Taylor shook his head. "I can do it. I just might need to rest every once in a while."

"No problem," Jake said. He hoisted the large backpack Skeet had given him onto his shoulders, and then he slung his smaller day pack across his chest. When his brother had done the same, they set off for Waterfalls Canyon.

The canyon was shaped like a big U, having been carved by glaciers thousands of years earlier. Without a hiking trail, the terrain proved difficult. The boys had to climb over rocks and hop across fallen logs and other obstacles. The dramatic view felt like the perfect backdrop for the drama they'd been through.

Even though the boys had spent several days on the edge of the Tetons, this was the first time they actually felt like they were going *into* them. Jake spun slowly around, taking in the jagged peaks, ice fields, and forests around them.

As they walked, however, the grade grew steadily steeper, and the stream began to curve to the right. Then they saw it—an enormous waterfall ahead.

"There it is," Jake said. "Columbine Cascade."

"Wow," said Taylor. "We're going to climb up that?"

"I guess we'll have to. This is where the map says he'd be."

"What if there's no one up there?"

Jake just looked into Taylor's eyes and shrugged. "We've come this far. There's no turning back now."

At the base of the falls, both boys craned their heads back, studying the rock formations.

"You think you can make it to the top?" Jake asked.

"I can make it," Taylor said, his jaw clenched with determination. "I say we go up the left side. It's steep, but not impossible. What do you say, Cody?"

Hearing his name, the dog barked and wagged his tail.

"Okay, then. Left side it is," said Jake.

The climb was a challenge. More than once, they had to help each other scramble up steep pitches and across slippery scree. Their route led them around and away from the waterfall itself.

"At least we don't have to go to Wilderness Falls. That's even higher up in the canyon," Jake said, gasping for breath.

Taylor was too weak to laugh, and they kept climbing.

Finally they reached the top. To their left, upstream, the water cascaded down in a series of shorter falls and drops, but to the boys' right, the water plunged in a dizzying fall of at least 150 feet. They stepped closer, and Jake shuddered looking at it.

"Man," said Taylor, also looking at what was almost a sheer drop. "Glad we're not going down *that*."

Suddenly a gruff voice said, "Don't be too sure."

24

The boys spun around. Dripping with sweat and with dried blood caked on his face, Bull stood in front of the boys, pistol in hand. Taylor let out a cry, and Jake drew in his breath—*he's alive!*

"Bull!" Jake exclaimed. "What the—?"

"You should have swung harder with that lamp," Bull sneered. "I always said you were no good at sports."

Suddenly Jake didn't have to worry if he'd killed Bull anymore—he was very much alive. Jake wasn't sure whether to be relieved or terrified. The boys took a step back. Cody stood his ground and growled.

"You better keep that mutt back or he takes the first bullet," Bull told them. Taylor quickly reached down to restrain the terrier.

"I was wondering when you three would show up," Bull continued. "You made me wait a long time."

"H-how'd you get here?" Taylor sputtered, looking as pale as when he'd faced the mama bobcat.

Bull held up some papers. Jake recognized one of them as his sketch from when he'd been trying to decipher his dad's clues, and the other as one of his dad's letters. "Turns out you're a better artist than an athlete," Bull said. "Between this and those directions your crazy father left, it didn't take much to figure it out. And the folk around here know all kinds of shortcuts they don't like to share with government types. All it took was a little *persuasion* and they were *happy* to help me . . . Apparently, you boys took the long way."

Bull stepped closer, reaching out for Jake's day pack with his free hand.

Jake and Taylor backed up to the water's edge.

Bull laughed. "Looks like you've run out of room this time, boys. It's up to you: die from a bullet or go over the falls."

Jake slowly began removing his backpack when a voice suddenly rang out, "Get away from them! Now!"

A tall man with long brown hair burst through a wall of shrubs behind Bull. Bull whirled, ready to fire his gun, but at the same moment, Cody leaped from Taylor's grasp and sank his teeth into Bull's ankle.

Swinging wildly, Bull fired, and the bullet ricocheted off

the nearby rocks. That was all that the tall stranger needed. He landed a right hook under Bull's chin, sending him reeling. But Bull's raw strength kept him from falling down, and he again raised his weapon to fire.

This time the stranger launched himself at Bull. Jake and Taylor heard ribs crack as Bull went down, his pistol clattering across the rocks and splashing into the rushing stream. But Bull was only stunned. He twisted the stranger off of him and threw his own punch, connecting with the other man's jaw. As the man fell back, he kicked Bull hard in the kidneys.

Bull gasped and fell face forward, but he also kicked out, hitting the stranger's stomach. Both men squirmed away from each other and staggered to their feet. Jake and Taylor looked on in bewilderment.

"I— I don't know who you are," Bull said, panting, blood dripping from his cheek. "But you're going to pay for this."

Again, Bull threw himself at the stranger, launching a devastating roundhouse kick. The stranger ducked just enough for the blow to glance off the top of his head, and the two men traded positions so that the stranger's back was now to the waterfall.

Bull grinned meanly. "Your meddling is through. Better say a prayer."

Bull lunged forward, but this time the stranger was ready. He sidestepped Bull, dodging the blow. Bull tried to stop himself, but the wet, loose shale might as well have been ice, and the missed punch threw him off-balance. With a cry, Bull tumbled forward into the fast-flowing stream. He desperately reached for a boulder next to him, and another rock on the other side, but his hands only skated across their wet surfaces. His eyes widened in terror, and he let out a piercing cry. Before anyone could react, the pounding white water seized Bull—and flung him over and into the falls.

Jake and Taylor stood at the edge of the cascading water. Finally Taylor reached out for Jake's hand, gripping it tightly. Jake turned to face the man who had helped them. He looked just as stunned as the boys.

He also looked familiar.

It wasn't the long hair or the wild unruly beard, or even the clothes—it was the eyes. Jake recognized them as his own. For a moment he didn't dare believe it, but the reality was too powerful to be ignored.

"Dad?"

Taylor also spun to meet the man's gaze. "What?"

The three of them stared at one another for a moment. The boys looked at each other in disbelief—they'd made it. They'd traveled halfway across the country, alone, against all the odds, and they'd found him.

The man, realizing the enormity of what he saw in front of him, simply held out his arms and motioned the boys forward. "Come here."

The boys rushed into their father's arms. None of them

said anything for several long minutes—none of them needed to. They were back together for the first time in years.

Finally the man pushed back. "Let me look at you. Are you both okay?"

Taylor nodded.

"Yes," Jake murmured, almost unable to take in the situation. Then "Yes!" he said more loudly, overcome with happiness.

The man quickly glanced at Taylor's leg. "What's this?"

"I had a bit of a run-in with a bobcat," Taylor replied.

"And that's just the beginning," Jake continued.

Abe Wilder's large hands squeezed the boys' shoulders, and tears began to slide down his cheeks.

"We'll get him patched up. The important thing is you . . . you came."

"How did you know we'd be here?" Taylor asked.

"I camp here every year. Did you get the letters I wrote? With the directions?"

"We got some letters," Jake said. "Did you write others?"

"I wrote one a year," their father said, "hoping they would reach you."

"Bull probably took 'em," said Taylor.

Their father's eyes darkened. "Was that Bull just now?"

Taylor nodded. "That was him—the no-good son of a—"

"He followed us out here," Jake said, cutting his brother off. "He's been living with us back in Pittsburgh, but he's only been after Mom's social security checks."

"Let's sit," Abe said. "You'd better tell me all about it."

The three of them and Cody sat on some moss-covered rocks away from the edge of the falls. Abe broke out some nuts, jerky, and dried berries, and while they ate, Jake and Taylor filled him in on the last several weeks—and years. Their father only interrupted occasionally to ask a question, and when they were finished, he shook his head. Again, tears spilled from his eyes.

"Boys, I am so sorry. I never meant to put you through all this. But I have to say that I'm proud of you. You've coped with more than any kids your age should have had to. In fact, I shouldn't even call you kids. What you've done goes beyond what many men could do."

"Well," Taylor said with a grin, "we also had the world's best dog with us."

Abe laughed and reached out to pet Cody. "That, you did." Then he grew serious again. "Your mother. Is she okay?"

Jake and Taylor glanced at each other.

"We don't really know," Jake said. "She was in the hospital when we left, but we were trying to find out when Bull caught us in town."

"Yeah," Taylor said. "Can we find out? Can we bring her here?"

By this time darkness had begun to fall. "We've got a lot of things to figure out, boys," Abe said. "I think we'd better camp here tonight. In the morning we begin a new life."

"You never told us about the valley," Jake said. "Did you really find it? Is it real?"

Even in the fading light, Jake could see the gleam of his father's smile. "Oh, I found it. It's a ways from here, near the border with Yellowstone. I found it not long after meeting up with your friend Skeet. I built a cabin there, and it's a place where we can all live."

The three of them spread their sleeping bags on a bed of moss thirty feet from the rim of the waterfall. They continued talking until Jake noticed a faint greenish wisp above Trapper Peak to the north. At first he thought that fatigue was making him see things, but the greenish wisps grew stronger and more elaborate.

"Ah, boys, the sky is putting on a show for us tonight," their dad said.

"What is it?" Taylor asked. "Some kind of lightning storm?"

"That, son, is the aurora borealis."

"The northern lights," Jake murmured, suddenly understanding.

"We're fortunate. It doesn't usually come so far south. It must be a good omen."

Jake just stared at the majestic sight above him and let out a contented sigh, unable to believe what he was seeing or who was sitting next to him. "It must be our lucky day."

WILDERNESS TIPS

The American Goldfinch

The American goldfinch is a small bird in the finch family, native to North America. Its huge migration range stretches from northern Alberta in the summer months, to southern Mexico in the winter.

Its most noticeable feature is its bright yellow plumage contrasted against its black wing and tail feathers. However, this bright contrast is only apparent in the males in the summer months; in the winter, they revert to a duller olive color. The female American goldfinch displays a slightly subtler yellow hue in summer, and molts to a similar tan-olive color in the winter.

The American goldfinch is the state bird of Iowa, New Jersey, and Washington.

The Wandering Garter Snake

The garter snake has a grayish color with dark spots and a light stripe running down the length of its back. These critters might look fierce but they aren't venomous—unlike rattlers (like the prairie rattlesnake and midget faded rattlesnake), which are much bigger, with brown spots down their backs.

Black Bear

The black bear usually tries to avoid humans and is *meant* to be less aggressive than the bad-tempered grizzly—but that doesn't mean it won't attack if it feels threatened or is desperate for food. Black bears have big claws on their hind legs and forelegs, small rounded ears, and thick black fur, although there are also different colors of bear across the country, from jet black to light brown and even to white.

Identifying Berries

 Huckleberry: Small and blue with a sharp taste . . . popular with bears!

 Raspberry: Bright red and delicious

 **Soapberry:** Not so tasty, as the name suggests, though it won't kill ya!

 Baneberry: Bright red, oval shaped, grows close to the ground. Eat too many and you're a goner. . . .

How to Build a Fire with a Magnifying Glass

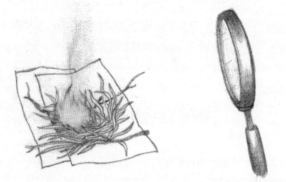

1. Gather tinder: grass, leaves, twigs, paper, or anything plant-based as long as it's very dry.

2. Build a nest out of the material and lay it on the ground.

3. Take your magnifying glass and angle it toward the sun until you make a small focused point of light.

4. Hold the magnifying glass in place until the tinder smokes and a flame develops.

5. Blow lightly on the tinder nest to nurture the flame, and add larger twigs and wood to create a bigger fire.

How to Build a Fish Trap

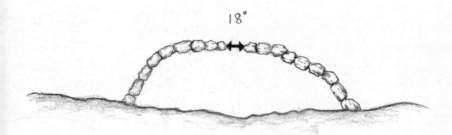

1. Gather rocks and make two curved fences in the water, facing upstream, from either side of the shoreline.

2. Leave a gap about eighteen inches wide in the middle.

3. Find bait to attract the fish. Throw it in and wait for the fish to bite.

4. Drop the final rock into the gap in the wall, trapping the fish. Then use a net to scoop it out of the water.

5. Have yourself a nice meal!

How to Set Traps

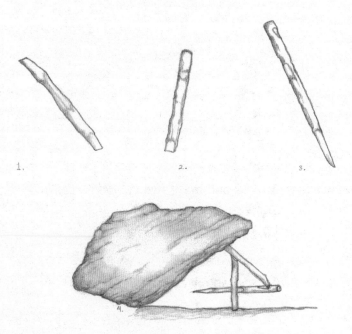

Skeet says all you need to catch yourself some dinner is three strong twigs, a post, a lever, and a trigger. . . .

1. Carve the post so one end looks like the chisel part of a flathead screwdriver, and carve a smooth facet into the middle to create a flat surface.

2. The lever stick is the diagonal part of the figure four. One end should be carved to look

like a chisel, and farther up, there should be a notch.

3. The trigger stick should be a little longer than the others, with a spiked tip for the bait. There should be two notches on the upper end of the stick.

4. Arrange the sticks in a figure-four formation, with a rock resting on the tip of the lever, and wait.

Using Medicinal Plants for Teatment

There are plants you can use for various treatments, and there are ones you should avoid. . . .

Larkspur: Grows two to four feet high and has blue and purple flowers. Toxic to humans, especially the seeds. Avoid.

Bitterroot: Low-growing flower with pink or purple petals. The roots are consumed by Shoshone and Flathead Indians as a delicacy. Some say they can stop bear attacks!

Oregon Grape Roots: Evergreen shrub with yellow flowers and dark blue-black berries. Used to treat upset stomach and inflamed skin.

Indian Paintbrush: Native to western America. The red flowers of the paintbrush are edible and sweet, and were eaten by some Native American tribes. However, avoid the roots and leaves, as these can be deadly!

Aurora Borealis: Northern Lights

I can't believe we finally saw the northern lights (and worked out what Dad was talking about when he mentioned aurora borealis.)! The whole thing was like a giant light show in the sky, with green and blue wisps snaking across the horizon. Dad reckons it's something to do with the sun's solar wind sending particles hurtling into the Earth's atmosphere at a funny angle. They normally happen much farther north—but I'm glad they made their way south this time!

Don't miss the Wilder boys' next adventure,
coming soon!

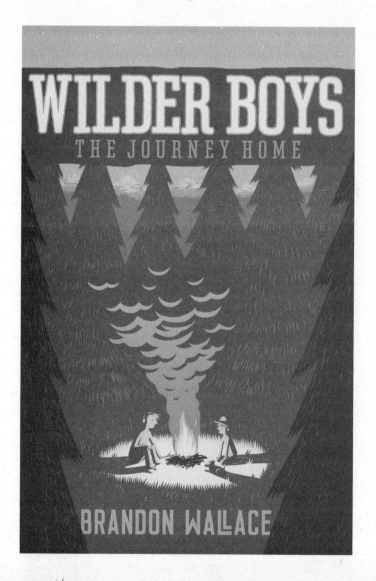